Praise for Acceptable Losses

"Acceptable Losses is a powerful story of three
lives joined yet isolated by personal struggles with
suffering, despair and loss. But, ultimately, it is also
a story of valor, survival and renewal. Norman
Weissman writes his compelling tale with a tide
of passionately descriptive language that pulls the
reader along by the sheer force of its inevitability. It
is an authentic work of art and terrible beauty."

Richard Geller, Author
"The Raspberry Man"

"Norman Weissman's first novel, Acceptable Losses,
is a haunting, powerful story about two sensitive,
urbane professionals who desperately try, but
ultimately fail, to accommodate the often conflicting
demands of alcohol and love. The prose is lean and
taut, yet simmering and passionate. Weissman's
keen insights into the true nature of love -- and
its close relationship to sacrifice and tolerance --
are almost frightening. His elegant, evocative prose
scintillates with paradox, eloquent tantrums and
absurd situations. Acceptable Losses is an exciting
page-turner that no reader will quickly forget."

Herman J. Obermayer, Author
"Soldiering For Freedom, A GI's Account of
World War II"

Praise For Acceptable Losses

"Acceptable Losses incisively dramatizes the redemptive power of feeling hearts overcoming life's inevitable losses. An overwhelming portrait of an alcoholic finding beauty amidst the lightning and thunder of a troubled mind."

Paul Shiman, Director
Newton Institute, Newton Massachusetts

"Acceptable Losses is a compelling narrative of afflicted, crumbling souls, punished for dishonoring the gift of creativity."

Norman Thomas Marshall, Co-Author
"John Brown: Trumpet of Freedom"

Acceptable Losses

Norman Weissman

Published in the United States by
Hammonasset House Books LLC
64 Edgecomb Street
Mystic, CT. 06255

Cataloging-in-Publication Data is available from
Library of Congress Control Number: 2007943111

Literary Fiction

ISBN-13: 978-0-9801894-0-7

FICO: 19000

Cover Painting By:
Poisson
22.3.51

www.hammonassethouse.com

Printed in the United States of America

For Eveline

ONE

Steve Irwin reluctantly awoke from a restless sleep and looked about his unkempt room. The wall-mirror made him look dissolute. He had not lived as slovenly since bachelor days. He would be happy to have his wife home again. He sat propped against the headboard and looked out the window to see a brightly painted tugboat pushing a string of overloaded barges, cascades of tumbling waves and pounding diesels fading as they moved downriver to New York, forty miles away.

Glancing at the sky he saw high cirrus foretelling an approaching front, and judging by scattered layers of stratus clouds, today would be bright and clear. A good day for her homecoming. A good day to make a fresh beginning. A good day to start a marriage anew. The glare of the sun on the water created a ribbon of light flowing between the highlands where the fog horn of a brick lighthouse sounded its mournful tones long after the mist had burned away. Across the river the hills flowed together each hollow and curve delineated by the soft morning light. Watching scattered wisps of fog settle in the valley he could see windows on the far shore reflecting the sun as daylight erased shadows on the granite cliffs.

He had seen sunrise and observed the weather in a daily ritual originating so far back in his past he could not remember when he first began watching each new day reveal itself to his wondering childlike gaze. Dawn never failed to evoke feelings of awe and expectation. It pleased him to watch the sun illuminate the Palisades across the river before leaving his bed and stepping into the shower. A pleasant beginning. Watching the sun rise and then the feeling of hot water spreading down shoulders and back, thawing and stretching muscles, luxuriating in the penetrating heat. Yes, this was a good time, if not the best time of day, and, as he turned off the water and dried himself, he could feel his flesh come alive and he paused remembering that morning long ago when he awoke and for the first time his wife was beside him, a woman of such beauty he trembled as he watched her sleep, a trusting child, head resting on one arm, her tanned body sprawled under the sheets. It was all promise then. Expectation. Love beyond his wildest imaginings now within his grasp if somehow he would reach out and find the courage to commit himself. He smiled and hung the towel on the rack to dry. Who could predict the future of an adoring smile?

He dressed quickly, donning a sweater before walking to the garage. He had a habit of leaning forward, bursting with animal energy as he walked, the bounce and swing of his body creating an appearance of power and compactness that made him seem shorter than his true height. Hunching over the typewriter had rounded his shoulders, thickening the sinews of his neck and when he stepped from his desk at the end of the day stretching his aching muscles, he looked upon his work as an ordeal. To endure and perhaps achieve something out of no other materials but himself was no small ambition, and he had learned that writing was an exhausting profession that consumed all that he had ever felt, thought, or seen in a lifetime dredging-up from his mind and spirit, his daily bread.

He drove slowly, following the post road along the river, knowing he had traveled this route before, reminded that this would be one more day of high expectations and renewed hopes. He had believed many things into existence. His career had no genesis other than his belief that he could do what he had been doing these many years, and this marriage was an expression of his faith that they could make something of their lives, and now that he no longer believed they were making anything of value he was possessed by a feeling of futility. This was not the first time he drove his wife home from this and other Sanitariums. And he knew it would not be the last. They lived a recurring cycle of in-and-out with only the names and faces of doctors changing whenever his wife willed one more alteration in behavior or location. Yes, it had taken him too many years to recognize the hatred masquerading in the diaphanous gowns of love.

He shifted gears climbing the high bluff overlooking the river, driving towards the large victorian mansion jutting against the sky, its faded white paint and overgrown grounds rundown as if all magic had fled from this mountain leaving only echoes of past glories and careers, autographed and framed under glass, gathering dust and curious glances in the hallway where the walls displayed photographs of the "celebrities" who had returned to the Limelight temporarily dried-out or tranquilized for their next encounter with reality.

He turned into the parking lot, switched-off the engine and glanced at his watch. He was early. He looked into the rear-view mirror and smoothed his hair, peering at a face that had grown thinner and more lined. His habitually questioning gaze, his way of intensely concentrating on people aroused doubt among those unaccustomed to looking at the world with genuine interest. He knew his interest in people made it seem he was asking something from them. Was it love? Or was it just knowledge that was expensive in time, money, and heartbreak? Now that he knew, more than he cared to know, about his wife, he realized how little he understood. In seeking the answer to her mystery he had missed what was before his eyes all the time.

They had been happy, their lives illuminated by a deep abiding love. Each day brought excitement and an unfolding passion bringing them together in sudden explosions of desire that convulsed them like reverberating shock waves. Their happiness was a broad, sweeping river that held them in its irresistible power. They told themselves, again and again, how fortunate they were to have met and fallen in love and to have had that love grow. Yes, they were committed, abandoning themselves to deep, true, overwhelming feelings. They were considerate, they were tender, they did what they could for each other and they delighted in a touch, a glance, a brief moment of silence when something deep within them stirred and reached out for communion. Their love grew more intense. They became demanding. Possessive. And now it all seemed like a dream one has difficulty remembering with the bitter taste of restless sleep its only residue.

He stepped from the car and nodded at her doctor waiting in the doorway, a tangled beard and graying hair flowing down to his shoulders. The Old Man. An old testament prophet shivering in a starched, white coat bulging with a thick fountain pen clipped inside his breast pocket. He could not resist smiling. The Old Man looked as if he had exhausted all the sorrow tracing lines across the parchment of a face glowing with kindness and wisdom. Steve valued their meetings in his cluttered office filled with books, diplomas, and dust. He healed with a word, a look, his voice enveloping patients in a warmth they had not experienced before. Steve followed him into the building, past the grim, unattractive receptionist who jabbed her finger under the desk, pressing the buzzer that unlocked the door leading to the narrow corridor where softly playing music accompanied the hum of overworked air conditioners. The Old Man opened his office door and gestured towards a chair as he sat behind his desk.

Steve had explained their happiness, knowing it seemed unreal, a fantasy. When speaking of the good years his words sounded hollow, and after many retellings he abandoned all effort to describe emotions that had long since atrophied. Today, there was nothing more for him to say.

"Your wife," the Old Man spoke slowly, leaning back in his chair, "your wife is anxious to return home." He opened a thick folder and turned the pages, "she has been eating and sleeping well, taking full advantage of the therapy we offer here." The

Old Man continued, his voice flowing in a calm, monotonous rhythm as if reciting a memorized elocution exercise whose subject was reassurance and confidence. Steve felt no compulsion to listen, the airy tones, and joyous lilt of the Old Man's words communicated the essence of the message. His wife would now be on her own. She would make her own future. As you know, all available therapies are unable to cope with alcohol. Take her home with our blessing and we'll hope for the best. The Old Man's voice was a musical performance, slow, stately passages of profound depth and meaning segueing into lighter, more melodic movements gradually building to a climax celebrating the beauty, charm, and extraordinary talent of this absolutely terrific woman and it was indeed a privilege, the Old Man said, his voice climbing to a final, swelling moment of dramaturgy, it was indeed an honor to be of some assistance to this troubled spirit. The cymbals did not clash nor did the drums roll as his voice continued its bouncy sing-song tones, fading into the natural rhythms of conversational speech. Steve heard these words and their softy playing music accompanied the hum of the overworked air conditioners. The Old Man opened his office door and gestured towards a chair as he sat behind his desk. Steve had explained their happiness, knowing it seemed unreal, a fantasy. When speaking of the good years his words sounded hollow, and after many retellings he abandoned all effort to describe emotions that had long since atrophied. Today, there was passion, his work. He had grown accustomed to long nights and cold beds and days filled with the satisfactions of his own creating.

She had awakened him. Or rather, they had

awakened each other, and, as he felt himself come alive, he looked back at the barren years with wonder. How did he ever live that way? Alone. So alone. A Monk in a cell. Hammering away at the words. He remembered reading a Camus quotation that stayed with him during that time.

"What a man's mind would accomplish, will be undone by his scrotum." These words no longer amused him.

He had met Helen Irwin at a casting session of one of his plays that ran four performances and closed to indifferent revues. She had waited patiently, seated at the back wall of the theater, keeping herself apart from the group of young actresses who stepped into center stage peering over the work lights, reading bits of flat, lifeless scenes that evoked increasing despair as they performed, smiling gallantly at rude rejection, and then exited to the wings, faceless, anonymous aspirants who converged on each new production with inexhaustible hope and limited skill. Helen walked into the spotlight, staring out at the increasing gloom, script in hand as she waited for the director to speak. She remained motionless, concentrating on the text, as if alone, the silence providing a background for a performance that began without a gesture, a movement or word to announce that a living, radiant character was now being created on stage. She waited calmly, the audience on the other side of the footlights staring at the tall, slender figure dressed in black, skirts covering her knees, barefoot on the un-swept boards littered with crushed cigarettes and candy wrappers. He could hear traffic in the street, and seats creaking, the director choking-back a cough as they watched her smile, eyes slowly rising from the script to look over the footlights, staring boldly at them, compelling attention as her mouth widened into a grin, then broadened to a full smile that illuminated her face, her eyes radiating a bright joy felt by the startled audience. Then she began reading, each word a distinct creation, each word a clear sharp assertion of the beauty and power of the human voice, each word a cry, an echo of her love for the speech filling the theater with a rhythm and life that continued growing as her voice lowered to a whisper, drawing them forward in their seats, straining to hear each nuance, each shading of intonation evoking and shaping emotions that flowed across the footlights, suddenly growing louder, more insistent as she finished reading, closed the script, and walked offstage, taking her magic with her.

She got this and many other parts, her career building slowly, opening and closing several plays that were distinguished by his workman-like energy and her performance. Steve and Helen were serious, disciplined and devoted to each other and their work, excluding everything from their lives but writing, acting and marriage. He maintained a reputation that brought neither fame nor fortune in plays and films that paid for their home overlooking the river, the first and only home that either of them had ever owned and been possessed by. Her drinking became more than a hazard of the trade as he worked longer and harder and drank less. She began destroying her fragile career, drinking and fighting and missing performances, her talent inadequate to pardon her behavior for though stardom has its privileges she was not a star nor indispensable to any production, and, as she became unemployable her drinking increased.

Her devotion to her appearance intensified.

Exercise, diet, and long hours apprenticed to a mirror maintained a beauty that flourished as the planes of her face thinned, her long, angular neck turning her head as if forever searching for the key light focused and scrimmed with no other purpose but to enhance and illuminate a profile that could have been famous had she remained before the public. Her look was created by a sharp, steady intelligence gazing at the world with knowing, almost cunning glances that happily merged in an overwhelming smile that projected her joy at being alive, on stage, facing an audience. She was Helen Irwin, she seemed to say, and though her nose was badly shaped and her mouth too large and her hair difficult to manage, something inside her transformed ungainly features into true beauty with only a little help from her hands. She had studied her face, analyzing its possibilities, passionately sculpting not in stone or clay but with tweezer and pencil, shadowing and shading flesh, emphasizing the folds of skin that gave her eyes an oriental, hooded look. Yes, he was caught up in the madness of her beauty. His obsession.

The Old Man continued. Case number such and such, a well-known face and name, prognosis indefinite, undetermined, diagnosis unanalyzed and probably un-analyzable, to be perfectly candid with you, my dear sir! The Old Man had the facts, all the episodes between the covers of a thick folder on his desk and he truly cared for this woman who was so many different women at one and the same time, with or without drink or love, or the devoted concern of her husband and doctor. Steve signed the release as the Old Man walked around the desk and opened the door.

"Good luck," the Old Man said, "and of course, should you ever need me, I'll make myself available." He escorted Steve down the corridor, the loudspeakers announcing the day's schedule of meals, games and television, soft music displacing the strident voice of the head nurse who attacked the silence with each announcement. He could not help thinking that the human voice mirrors and distinguishes the soul, the unforgettable voices of presidents, actors and people expressing their uniqueness more powerfully than their eyes. He would never forget this voice, precise, brittle, orderly, so without doubt, contrasting with Helen's little-girl's voice that seemed helpless and weak when once it had been the most vivid color of her flamboyant personality.

Following the Old Man he passed locked doors concealing mystery and tragedy not dispelled by music. Who lived behind these doors could only be imagined. Survivors of shock treatments, basket weaving, play therapy, and Saturday night dances for patients and hopeful visitors who parked their sense of reality at the door, entering a make-believe world made dreary by streaked lipstick and shrill laughter rising over the dance floor like flotsam surfacing through layers of pain and terror.

The Old Man unlocked the door to the visitor's lounge admitting Steve. Helen's luggage was at the entrance. He knew that room well. Rows of magazines precisely tabled, overlapping in parallel stacks, each issue revealing the masthead of the previous month's copy flanked by polished ash trays and chairs precisely angled under a reading lamp.

Christ! How little anyone knows. Yes, he did see Helen's problems many years ago. In his wallet he carried a photograph taken when she was eight. A thin, long-limbed girl crouching at the edge of the sea, one knee pressing into wet sand, clasped hands digging a hole that quickly filled with water, head tilted back, looking into the camera, mouth grim, as if startled by a threatening intruder, and he remembered being shocked by the look in her eyes in the photograph when first she gave him the picture, for she was not a child playing on a beach but rather a frightened animal cornered in her lair. A picture of innocent terror he would never forget and the first hint of fears to come. He always carried that photo, studying it in search of mysteries forever beyond his understanding, and though she grew taller, and added flesh to that thin body, the beautiful woman she became, forever looked out upon the world through fear-stricken eyes.

He had recognized the core of her being in the photo, and had denied his insightful grasp of who she was. It was more than he was prepared to live with at that, or any other time, and so he had waited many years before marrying. Watching his feelings grow from a seed of doubt and hesitation, he fell in love blindly, knowing he was blind, obsessed, ignoring the evidence of her distress every time he looked at that picture.

He picked up the suitcases and carried them to the car, stowing them carefully, and when he returned to the building Helen was leafing through the pages of Vogue, and when she turned towards him he again saw the startled young child on the beach, the fear in her eyes abruptly transformed into a look of pleasure as he leaned over and kissed her cheek. He noticed her dress hanging loosely, her face lean and hard.

"You've lost weight," he said, "seems like I've

married a teenager, by God!" He looked her over. A hungry look. A leer without the whistle.

A hint of a smile acknowledged his tribute. Helen hesitated, considering her reply. Opening lines established the tone of all her best scenes. Today was important.

"You like me this thin?" she asked, her long, graceful fingers touching her hair in a familiar gesture. "With my boobs, I'd never be taken for a fashion model. Never."

He laughed. She really is her old self. "Very becoming," he said, arms opening in a welcoming embrace which she did not enter. Yes, it was too soon. Give her time, he told himself. The flesh that was once one and indivisible was now separate, estranged. The bond that had so passionately locked them together now tenuous. Yes, give her time.

She stepped back. Withdrawing. Suddenly angry.

"The food was incredible. They kept firing cooks, each one worse than the last one they fired. Last week I didn't eat a thing. Not a mouthful." She patted her flat stomach. Point made. He held the door, and then they walked slowly towards the car, her legs unsteady, and he was grateful no one insisted on a wheelchair. When she slid into the front seat he leaned over and kissed her again. A proper little girl kiss. Without passion. Two people who once knew each other. Very well. Very well indeed.

"I missed you," he said. The truth.

"Good," she answered. "I'm glad."

He drove slowly, the road crowded with school buses stopping at intersections, trucks and cars patiently waiting until the flashing red lights turned off. He accelerated up the familiar winding road towards home remembering her seated next to him, her thigh pressed lightly to his, the countryside flowing past in a changing panorama of beauty, the two of them singing and talking, endlessly talking, her hand resting in his lap.

"I see your driving hasn't improved."

"Nervous?"

"As a cat."

He slowed, rounding the curve on top of the hill and when he glanced at her he saw she was staring out the window, studying the flat, windless river, the sun glaring on the water. She reached into the glove compartment and put on a pair of dark glasses. She loved wearing dark glasses. And riding with him in a car.

"May I have your autograph?" he asked.

"I'm only a housewife, sir. No one famous."

"Is that what you want?"

"Yes. That is all I want."

He turned into the side road leading off the highway, driving through woodlands and meadows, passing groves of birch trees budding into leaf. The forest smelled damp from last night's rain.

"Spring," she said.

"The wettest in ten years."

"Did you get much work done?"

"There was nothing else. Work, and listening to the rain."

"It's good to be home."

"I know."

She was leaning against the head rest, staring out the window, and he reached out to hold her hand. He could feel tension dissipate as she turned and smiled as if to touch the world with a promise.

"Last time," she said. "Never again."

"I hope so."

She smiled and turned to the window and he could feel her pulse quicken, her fingers clasped in his, squeezing hard, and suddenly she seemed old, the lines around her eyes sagging as she studied her brooding reflection in the glass. She noticed him watching and suddenly she resumed her bright, hopeful face. Her tomorrow face.

"That's better," he said.

That's the way it will always be, he thought. Her expression changing with each mood, no matter what he said there was no way of anticipating her reaction. No way of preventing sudden descents into depression or flights of euphoria.

"What was it like?" he asked.

"This time it was wallpaper," she said. "They had this pukey-green colonial design that repeated every other panel and when I woke in the morning the first thing I saw was this mismatched sheet sprouting a church steeple out of a cow's ass. Sears Roebuck surrealism out of Salvador Dali. Did you hear that Musak?"

"Yes."

"And the head nurse? Every night, at midnight, in a voice like sandpaper she called for piss in a bottle! Sleep and piss. Piss and sleep. Christ I was bored. Couldn't read or listen to any decent music. Everybody laughing all the time at God knows what. A bunch of hyenas. Just four walls, a window, and a door that rattles in its frame every time some heavy footed elephant walked past. And when the food cart rolled by on wheels not oiled in twenty-five years, I jumped right out of my skin! Speaking of torture,

Amnesty International should do something about this place! The bell rings, you get up. The door opens and you eat. They hand you a bottle and you piss! Christ! They tested my urine fourteen times a day!"

"To protect your kidneys."

"It's my liver. You got it all wrong. They're trying to regenerate my liver so it will purify my rich, juicy red corpuscles. Did you pay the bill?"

"Of course."

She smiled her charming smile. Her voice rising. "Con men with doctor's degrees turning everybody into vegetables! The Old Man is so dull. He's got an identity crisis. I really gave that man something, you know that? He says I have uncanny insight into what makes people tick. He wants me to study psychology. You know, what's the sense of wasting all these years on the couch? He knows all the shortcuts to a degree! But it's not for me. I could never sit and listen to that garbage from people's minds. That's why shrinks are suicidal. Highest incidence of any profession. I think he's madly in love with me. You know we really talk! He's truly amazed at the insights I give him. It's quite a responsibility having someone in love with you. It's a sacred trust what's between a therapist and patient. Privileged information! Not even the FBI could get that man to breath a word. He's so moral it's disgusting. Some good woman should climb into his bed. He's too goddamn shy to ask. I didn't want him to fall in love with me. No way! It's just that he's so lonely."

He rounded the curve and climbed the hill leading to the white stucco house on the point, the broad river sweeping past the rocky peninsula evoked a feeling of homecoming. Helen leaned forward in her seat, restless, eager to arrive. He parked in the driveway and removed the luggage.

"Welcome home," he said.

They walked through the garden to the back door, Helen, with a forlorn look, examining the flowers bordering the footpath. Her flowers. Her children.

"Must have been one hell of a winter," she said.

"It was."

"Garden's dead."

"It won't take you long to get it right."

"I wouldn't know where to start."

They entered the house, Steve carrying the suitcases upstairs, placing them on an unmade bed, and when he returned to the kitchen water was boiling on the stove.

"I don't see how anybody can live this way," she said, rinsing two cups in the sink, drying with a tattered dish towel as the kettle whistle shrilled. She turned off the flame, added coffee and slowly stirred the brew. "A cleaning lady rearranging the dust once a week is not enough."

"Apparently."

They walked into the living room, Helen sitting gracefully on the sofa, placing her cup on the coffee table, leaning against thick cushions, back straight, glancing around the room as if she was an elegant character in a long-running play.

"You didn't spend much time in this room."

"It's too big and lonely."

She smiled indulgently. "The only clean room in the house." She watched him place a log in the fireplace.

"You've lost weight."

"I thought you'd like it."

"I do. You look years younger."

He placed kindling and paper under the log and struck a match. The flames curled, enveloping the dry wood as he shoved an iron poker against the log, exposing the dry underside to the fire. He turned and looked at her. She was staring into her cup, cradling it between both hands, the steamy vapors rising as she swirled the coffee in a circular motion. He poked the fire. She looked up, suddenly ravaged, desolated. He had seen that expression before. Many times. All of them bad.

"For God's sake all I really ask is to let me be me! That's all! Me! I want to be me! Why is it so God damn hard? Is there something wrong with my being myself? God damn it to hell anyway If I can't be me I don't want to be anybody else! Come hell or high water I am going to be myself no matter what the hell you do I am going to be the best God damn me you've ever seen. I just want to be me!"

"Let's not talk about that right now," he said, walking to the window, opening the blinds, the sun slanting into the room, illuminating specs of dust wavering in the light.

"You think it's easy being me? You think I'm having a ball? You, without a nerve in your body, do you know what it's like hurting so bad you can't stand it anymore? Hurting so bad you can't breathe! Believe me there's hurt inside some people can drive them out of their skulls and until you're in their heads you have no right saying anything about anyone in that kind of agony. There's something squeezing you so tight you want to die. Christ! You and this house are driving me up the wall. I walk in the door and I can't breathe! I'm suffocating. The walls are closing in. I'm trapped."

TWO

Yes, thirty years ago was a time when drink was the focus of Steve Irwin's life. He remembered sitting on the edge of the hospital bed feeling the damp floor underfoot sending chilling shivers through his body as he stared through bloodshot eyes across the alcoholic's ward listening to other drunks mumbling in the dark, hearing outside the locked door, a nurse sprawled over a desk, stirring in his sleep, clearing his throat, snoring. Steve listened to no other sounds, nothing to feel but the cold, nothing to look at but the darkness, nothing to remember but the blessed, cooling, liberating, long-fingered touch of scotch, or even that of the cursed wine.

Steve Irwin's thirst.

Dear Mother of God how easily it began. Brandy and milk three times a day. Nourishment to carry-on, with other foods rising in his throat impelled by that sometimes severe, sometimes moderate spasm of the sphincter muscle of the pylorus at the far end of the stomach where the duodenum awaits its thrice daily ration. Brandy and milk, warmed, imbibed to sustain where more substantial items were regurgitated.

But what use food when scotch was available? The controlled utilization of scotch, a habit that kept him flying forty-four months, but later proved inadequate to the demanding task of keeping Steve Irwin alive long after the last sphincter muscle of the pylorus spasmed a last and farewell spasm. Yes, long after those pyloric gates opened the habit of eating solid foods had been obliterated by the liquid which brightened his perceptions and dulled his fears. Steve Irwin's thirst. Alcohol, gasoline, and nitroglycerin mixed in exact proportions propelling high compression engines, steadying his hands and sharpening his eyes, for how many years? At ten gallons per hour, how many gallons, in how many hours? Yes, how many victories? How many defeats? How many deaths?

The answer? Only one.

Man's work. To drink. To fornicate. To fly. No more complicated than that. Or was it? Was this matter of being a man that simple? Merely a job of taking what ever it was you had to take off that rolling deck? Or drifting through a curve? Or pressing a trigger. Or squeezing a woman's breast? Or laying a stick of bombs across a bridge? Or simply, just getting laid? Simplicity itself. So what's complicated? You either win or lose. Victory or death! That's the spirit. Steve Irwin's spirit. If you can't grab the little brass ring, stay the hell off the merry-go-round. There's no mister-in-between, ever. No. Not in this life, not in this game. You either won, and kept winning, or you were dead without knowing the truth about yourself. So why the hell don't you just get up out of this ward and quit? Grow up! Time to live what ever remains of your life. Time to find out if you really can be a man, an ordinary guy who comes home at five o'clock every night and takes one drink, dinner, and his wife, in that order. Something you've never done and probably never will do. Surviving boredom requires guts, and that is one item you have always lacked. The courage to live an ordinary life. The whole ball of wax, gift wrapped in monotony, sanctified by the church, blessed by children. One wife, one life, one catastrophe.

Steve peered through the wired glass window in the door watching the nurse sleeping at the table near the elevator. Steve rapped on the glass. The nurse grunted. Steve watched him shuffle towards the door.

"Yes?"

"A glass of water please".

The nurse walked to the water cooler across the hall. He filled a paper cup and drank slowly, luxuriating as the cool liquid slaked his parched throat. Refilling the cup, he returned, fumbling with a key ring before opening the door.

"Thanks buddy," Steve said.

The nurse grinned, handing the cup to Steve who drank in a long, breath-holding swallow.

"So drink jug-a-lug, jug-a-lug," Steve sang hoarsely. "How about a cigarette?"

Reaching into his pocket the nurse offered Steve a cigarette and match, pausing a moment to watch Steve's first deep, contented drag. "Now, now, now. Now would be the time to take this friendly little bastard," Steve told himself. "Take him and the Goddamn keys." Just one side-arm slash across the bridge of the nose... "Gentlemen, your weapons are nature's own... first, the side of the hand, blinding your opponent, shattering the bones, then the cupped palm, upward thrust with the heel of the hand jamming the sharpened cartilages into the sinus cavity and brain whereupon death ensues, instantly? Yes gentlemen, your weapons are indeed nature's own. The eye-gouging thumb, the slashing side of the hand, the upthrust palm, the quaint, and highly overrated fist, the paralyzing backward jabbing elbow, the butting head, the upthrust knee to the groin, the stomping foot scraping down the shinbone, nature's great gifts and indeed the greatest of all, gentlemen, never hesitate to use your fangs. Bite deep with a twisting motion gentlemen, separate the jugular and thirty seconds later your great natural endowments, the weapons we carry naked into this world will insure your survival.

Any questions? Remember. He who hesitates is lost. But definitely."

"Thanks friend," Steve said aloud to the nurse. The nurse nodded and said nothing. Steve watched him return to the table and sprawl into a chair. The cigarette smoke was dry in Steve's throat, his hand trembled as he raised the butt to his lips, heart pounding, blood throbbing in his ears, he felt dizzy and turned away from the window, staring into the darkness, his breathing returning to normal as the adrenaline of fury subsided. He could not attack this man. No, not for all the booze in the world. He smiled. Things were looking up. Yet it was only drink that could dispel the distant sound of a low-throated chattering propeller changing pitch in a black tropical night smelling of orange blossoms, salt air, and the feel of warm wind pressing a sweat-dampened flight suit to trembling skin. Did anyone really think about that death then? Removed from our midst, one sweet smile, one voice now silent; those tap dancing feet will never again jig across the barracks floor; for he is ashes now, rather a smoke-blackened cinder hanging inverted from a bucket seat transformed into the pure white dust of melted aluminum and magnesium. Pure white dust blanketed with fire-quelling foam that did not extinguish, did not suffocate flames turning a delightful spirit into a memory. What the hell was his name? After all these years, what was his name? Who will remember anything but that he was always writing letters, forever reverberating shower stalls with high-pitched song, words and melody surviving long after his death, emerging from how many radios, how many record players, to evoke, in how many minds the thought that once I knew a guy who sang those words. Ridiculous songs. Sentimental lyrics. Yet, inexplicably, why should they retain such beauty, evoke such emotion? The landing signal officer frantically beat the air with fluorescent paddles, the "Talker" pleaded into a deadened microphone, "one wheel down... one wheel down...", the signalman aimed his light-gun, transmitting red flashes into the concentrated vision of a pilot focused on a perspective of hooded lights outlining two hundred feet of runway. "Wave-off... wave-off... wave-off!" screamed the "Talker", the LSO pleading, "come on son, get your head out of your ass," the pilot throttling back, the aircraft settling, touching one wheel, one wingtip, its tail-hook failing to engage a restraining wire, digging a spinning prop into the macadam before cart-wheeling into the darkness, the sound of ripping metal somehow triggering the high-pitched wail of a crash truck siren chasing a finger of flame into the night. The red signal rocket exploded overhead, closing the field, now spreading a small lake of flames, spectators crowding its shores, watching an asbestos clad rescue team swinging axes in the inferno, slashing at aluminum, prying back the crushed canopy, attempting to rescue the pilot cradled, head down, in his shoulder straps, watching them struggle towards him with unseeing eyes, or was it a smile, one arm dangling in helpless greeting? Steve restrained an impulse to raise his arm, to reply to that lifeless form disappearing in the flames. He stood there unable to move, wordlessly encouraging the spreading blanket of foam choking the fire, allowing darkness to mercifully conceal death.

What was his name? After all these years is it important? Why remember? Why not forget? Why not forget the memory of standing in the dark, throats dry, clenching and unclenching our fists in helpless rage, watching stumbling figures silhouetted against the flames, jack-knifing the wreckage, gently lowering the blackened corpse onto a canvas tarp that was folded over how many times? Why remember the slow walk to the mess hall, the green linoleum-covered tables repellent in the florescent light, the mess cooks standing silently behind the food counter, for they had also heard the siren, seen the flames, fed, three times each day, that wink, that grin, never failing to promote, a larger serving, a second helping, a returning smile? The young pilots circled the table, sliding their trays, holding mugs of coffee at their lips, inhaling its steam and the aroma of food, never once speaking of death, for before their eyes was an image of themselves, blackened bundles wrapped in canvas, bouncing in the rear of a pick-up truck, driving slowly to the morgue. They thrust into their mouths servings of eggs and steak and potatoes, fat chunks of bread vanishing as if to compensate for the acquisition of knowledge that would never vanish, never disappear, never be drowned by the eating and drinking and other pleasures of how many lifetimes?

THREE

Helen Irwin thrust her head under the pillow awakened by the rhythmic pounding of the typewriter. The tac-a-tac-a-tac-a-tic-tac-ting propelling the carriage across its rails reverberated with a metallic thunk penetrating her overstrained psyche, each key stroke striking sharp blows on her sensitized nerve endings. She pressed the pillow around her ears as the grating sound of a new page slipped behind the roller became prelude to an irritating silence. Yes, it was cruel, the moment she found the rhythmic pattern a soothing hypnotic introduction into a deeper sleep she would be awakened by irritating pauses that found her welcoming the next burst of energy bringing that infernal machine alive. Chattering and silence. Twin tormentors as she willed herself into a restless half-conscious sleep driven by distant furies. The pillow felt hard under her head and the twisted bedclothes pressed across her back as she covered her eyes under the blanket shielding them from the grey light edging under the window shade. Then an all-pervading cloud of sleep returned as she raised her knees up against her abdomen and thrust her thumb into her mouth.

The warmth spread, and in tonight's dream she hummed a simple childhood tune accompanied by small porcelain figures revolving on top of a music box. A violinist and his lady turned and bowed to each other as the music continued. Then the violinist's mouth opened in simulated song as his lady gracefully bowed turning and dancing on the music box. The violinist continued singing as the platform rotated and sweeping his arm down to his feet he danced from view as the top of the music box slowly turned in time to Helen's continued humming, her rhythm slowing as the platform stopped rotating. Now she recognized that the music box was blue and white with gold trim, and in her dream it became a large granite house surrounded by a snow-covered lawn and it was early morning with the first slanting rays of the winter sun casting long shadows behind linden trees that hid the house from the street. The front door opened. A naked child stepped out into the snow and began running around the house. Once, twice, three times the child circled the mansion, and then, cold, and exhausted, the child knocked on the door, her small fists striking wood, enormous sobs convulsing her shivering body. Then, after more anguish, the door opened.

Helen Irwin sat up in bed and swung her legs down on to the floor feeling the cold wood underfoot as she groped with her toes for a pair of overstuffed wool slippers. Sliding her feet into them she sat on the edge of the bed and looked down at the grain pattern etched on alternate planks of flooring laid from wall to wall in thin and then wide bands of varnished oak. The morning light was dull from a high overcast that covered the winter sun and she raised her eyes searching out the small digital clock that tumbled time with an endless succession of numbers that soundlessly whirred past each moment. There were no seconds, no rhythmic tic-toc that made each alternate swing of the pendulum a syllable of loss. Only an inaudible hum, a gentle click as each new number revealed itself. The emotion of her dream remained with her as she counted the hours and minutes irritated by the sound that propelled her existence forward to the next moment when she stood up on the cold, hardwood floor. Blood drained from her head, her vision graying as she tottered on trembling legs, reaching out to the bedpost, grasping the polished mahogany as the pounding of her heart quickened. She looked down at the bed table at the crumbled cigarette package and blackened ashtray with its nightly accumulation of butts. A sour morning taste followed by painful coughs as she held on to the bed, her vision dimmed with each effort to clear her breathing passages. Opening the drawer, her hand groped inside and thrust a cigarette between her lips. She walked to the window, to a book of matches that fit into her palm as she lit her cigarette, inhaled, and waited for trembling to cease.

Anxiety attacks often emerged from the emotions of a dream and she felt fear as a series of small shocks that left her weak and threatened and unable to breathe. Tremors of terror evoked a sense of disaster unseen, impending, hanging over each waking moment like a cloud of feeling that had no other shape, no other dimension than an ever-present dread that was the only color, the only texture, the only content of her mornings. Fear was poison, unreasoning, unnamed, unattributed anxiety that tightened inside her like a giant hand making her suddenly rigid, unable to swallow, her stomach taut and unyielding as she tasted the dry, hard helplessness that was her daily portion of misery. It was not a steady, unremitting feeling, but a pressing down into despair that plunged her to darker depths with each new surge, drowning in black thoughts until the pain intensified and there was no scream, no cry for help, no desperate prayer that relieved the weight paralyzing her. She raised the curtain, and inhaled, staring out the window at the grey light that enveloped the trees in a gauze-like mist that distorted their silhouettes into grotesque shapes. She studied these giant prehistoric creatures stretching long angular necks down to the water and again she felt transported to a domain of terror far beyond the bearable edge of despair.

Helen jabbed the cigarette into an ashtray and turned from the window to the door where a loose hasp rattled as she walked on the hardwood floor. She bent over to pick up a wad of cardboard wedging the folded shape into the door jamb. Leaning against the door she turned the lock, pulled the knob, determining that the door was secured. Not a sound creaked from the door frame as she returned to the closet. She stepped on to a chair under the shelf, and reaching behind a hat box her hand grasped the smooth surface of a bottle. She paused to listen to the rhythmic pounding of the typewriter, and then she looked down at the floor, at the alternating widths of polished oak that reflected light in a dazzling bright blinding flash. She swayed on the chair reaching out to steady herself against the wall, closing her eyes as equilibrium returned and then, with a stab of courage she stepped down, clutching the bottle to her breast. She rested a moment as her legs steadied, walking to an empty glass on the bureau. Sitting on the floor she poured a drink. She raised the glass to the light, inhaled the fumes, and drank with a long, comforting sigh. She sat cross-legged on the hard wooden floor her arms embracing her knees, her head inclined to one side listening to distant sounds that she followed with ferocious concentration. The sounds intensified as she moved her head from side to side following an inaudible rhythm that slowly increased in tempo. She closed her eyes and pressed her lips together, her face tense, the hard lines of her mouth turning white as the blood receded and her jaw jutted out in apparent anger, overt rage. The tempo increased, and the movements of her head accentuated the heavy beat of the insistent music that she followed with catatonic jerks. Her head swung from side to side with abrupt movements and her long flowing hair tumbled down her back reaching her waist as she swung her head ever faster as the rhythm quickened. Then she began to hum, as if in a dream, and as the music grew louder in the caverns of her mind she suddenly stiffened and threw her head back, her hair swaying to unheard rhythms like a living metronome of silken beauty. The humming grew louder, and suddenly her movements changed as she began rocking back and forth on her haunches, swinging forward and back as the music reached a strange and savage climax that illuminated her face with an expression of childlike vulnerability. The inaudible music played faster and now she swung her head from side to side as she rocked forward and back humming an unvarying melody of one single note that seemed to rumble up from some inner reservoir of agony that could be emptied in no other way. The humming filled the room, and her long dark hair propelled by the swinging of her head lengthened the arc of its movements across the small of her back as she continued rocking, the music now furious, the humming increasing in pitch until a single shrill note pierced the gloom. Then with a furious thrust forward she toppled on to the floor, arms outspread, hair flying over her shoulder as her head struck the polished wood and the insistent rhythms of the music continued louder and more compelling as she began pounding her forehead against the shimmering brightness with savage determination that brought her head crashing down again and again, her long dark hair falling forward, covering her face, cushioning each blow as the unvarying notes of dreadful music impelled her on to a compulsive reaching out for oblivion. The humming continued, the rhythmic accompaniment of the pounding intensified until with one final groan of exhaustion she collapsed, entering a silence so deep, so profound as to flood her entire being with stillness and peace.

FOUR

Steve Irwin listened to the rhythmic pounding and turned to watch the hills across the river disappear into the overcast. The thumping on the floor above stopped. He looked up at the ceiling anticipating the next sound. The silence persisted. He thrust another page into the typewriter. The clouds darkened. The first slash of rain creased the window distorting the landscape into fantastic images. The rain pattered on the roof as water coursing down the panes blurred the glass. He felt helpless fear as he thought of Helen. On the window the first wind-eddies created rivulets that obscured his vision and then a recurring thought overwhelmed him. She was going to die. She was pursuing death. He was her accomplice in self-destruction.

Now he turned to another window, watching water flowing across the glass and the terror of another moment returned as the rhythmic sweep of windshield wipers alternately cleared and obscured his vision as he peered over the steering wheel searching for the edge of a narrow black-topped road illuminated by mud-splattered headlights. The wheel felt cold in his hands. The car swayed as the wind crossed the salt marshes slanting the heavy rain of an approaching northeaster. He wiped condensation from the windshield and strained to follow the road as the storm blotted out visibility with heavy wind gusts that pressed against the side of the car. Helen slumped in her seat, leaning against the door, staring out the rain-spattered windows. She lit a cigarette, the match flare illuminated her face. Her hair puffed up over one shoulder, her head bobbed with the undulating movement of the car. She lit a second match, igniting the filter tip, tasting the burning cardboard, replacing the charred, unsmokable end with a fresh cigarette that hung between her lips as she raised the flame. She leaned forward, inhaling deeply, jamming the match into the ashtray.

"Please sit back, Helen."

"You bastard." She waved the cigarette. "You are a bastard," she said.

A lull in the storm cleared visibility as he followed the road bordering the perimeter of the airport. The blinking red approach lights on top of telephone poles appeared for a moment and then the rain again obscured the road. He drove through a grove of pine trees feeling the tension rising in Helen as she exhaled acrid smoke filling the car with the odor of burnt tobacco. She sat erect, hand clutching the arm rest, her head bobbing with the dips and heaves of the road.

"Just one more dance. One more lousy dance," she said.

He did not reply.

"You know how I love to dance."

The road turned and passed between dark

sentinels of pine illuminated by headlights. He shifted gears as they climbed the hill on the ridge overlooking the bay.

"One Goddamn lousy dance."

"It was time to leave."

She lit another cigarette, the reflected flare blinding him. He slowed, waiting for night vision to return. He dimmed the dashboard lights.

"That Goddamn floor was slippery."

"I know."

"I slipped," she said. "That's all."

He recalled the thunderous crash of dishes and silverware, a table overturned, waiters scurrying to assist her to her feet, Helen entangled in a broken chair, sitting on the floor, afloat in crockery, rejecting offers of aid, dignified despite embarrassment and confusion as if this unfortunate incident was the most amusing event of a delightful evening. He could not restrain a smile.

"What the hell are you smiling about?"

"Nothing."

"The hell you say!"

She wiped condensation from the window as the storm abated, the rain and mist disappearing as the road climbed above the fog. She inhaled a quick series of puffs, shifting in her seat as he drove faster. Riot and rage, he thought. Her mood was set for a spell of riot and rage and a feeling of helplessness returned and saddened him. If only he could get her home in time. He recognized her rising tension as she inhaled, her lips and cheeks pursing, nostrils flaring as she sucked the cigarette dry. She needs a drink, fast.

He was a student of her alcoholic consumption. Observed drinking, that is. Her unobserved drinking he could only estimate trying to read from apparent effects, speech, eyes, smile, the movement of her head and body yielding clues to secretive behavior. Her curve of rising tension was consistent. The first out-croppings of anger never appeared with just a few drinks.

"How about a smoke?" he asked.

She extended her arm, his eyes concentrating on the road, he took the cigarette by the offered end, the ignited end, thrusting the hot, burning ash between his lips, the searing pain bringing tears, blinding him as he spat out the burning stub. The car slewed to the edge of the road, and then, vision clearing, he regained control. A wave of agony spasmed his cheek radiating from the burn on his lip.

"That was stupid," he said.

"You never watch what you are doing."

He wet the burn on his lip, the pain subsiding. Yes, she was heading towards riot and rage, but not until they arrived home. A knot inside her tightened, the rhythm of her drinking interrupted by this drive, and yes, she would have been better dancing away this explosion of energy to achieve an equilibrium, a balance arrived at by dancing and drinking in equal measure, converting fury into the movements of dance. He was wrong to bring her home. But the cold stare of the headwaiter was unmistakable.

What went on inside of her, he could only guess. As the speed of the car increased she cranked down the window and the wet salt air displaced smoke. She thrust her face into the breeze closing her eyes as the rain drops splattered her cheeks.

"That's delicious," she said.

She moved her head, offering each cheek to

the flow of air. Her tension reached a plateau. She needed another drink. Without one, her rising anger could neither explode in one fantastic discharge of emotional lightning or subside into drunken stupor. Her struggle for balance, for equilibrium had been frustrated by getting her into the car, confining her to a seat with every nerve and muscle raging for violent physical action. She cranked the window closed and leaned back in her seat.

"I feel marvelous," she said.

She spoke in her little girl's voice. "I'm sorry about that cigarette," she said.

"I know."

"Let's go back. It stopped raining."

"We're almost home."

"I want to go dancing. I must go dancing," she said, her voice trembling in a babyish tone. "Please."

It was worse in summer. The long days on the beach, the sun dehydrating her tanned body intensified the effects of drink. Her inner furies recharged energies accumulated during hours of physical inactivity. Tension and rage ignited by a hot sun stirring emotions that each night achieved a critical mass detonated by alcohol. What that explosive mass was, was uncertain. Catalyzed by booze something within her compressed her energy into surges of emotion seeking release. With each drink she struggled to alleviate this ever-increasing pressure. Helen drank for deliverance.

"It's Saturday night. The band plays until two," she said. She reached across the car touching his arm. "Let's turn back."

He could now see lights across the bay. The storm was moving out to sea. Inside the car he could feel a thunderhead rising, the touch of her hand transmitting violence, her expanding universe of rage contained and tonight hopefully confined within her thin, trembling body. Her shoulders began to shake. Angrily she stabbed the half-smoked cigarette into the ash tray.

"Just a few minutes, and we'll be home," he said.

She began rocking back and forth in the seat. He drove faster, the road running straight through the pine forest bordering the bay, the first stars appearing as a low scud of clouds dispersed, the wind shifting, blowing off-shore. The night breeze. His hands clutched the wheel as she slammed her fist down on the arm of the seat.

"I don't know about you," she said, "But I'm going dancing!"

He heard the click of the latch and with an abrupt movement the door opened, Helen pushing with all her strength against the pressure of the wind, forcing her body out of the car, shoving against the door, fighting the wind with a desperate surge, both arms pressing outward, the rush of air streaming her hair back, covering her face as she struggled, Steve grabbing her arm, one hand grasping the steering wheel, his eyes on the road, his foot stabbing at the brake, her enormous strength pulling him to her seat, the steering wheel his only anchor as the car swerved across the highway towards the pine trees flowing past the wavering beams of headlights. He pulled against her with a fierce spasm of strength, his arm trembling, steering the car back towards the middle of the road as she pulled outward, his foot stabbing for the brake as the car swerved towards the embankment, towards a row of pine trees, the door opening wider as the wind pressure decreased, the car slowing as his foot searched for the brake, struggling to stay on the road, his grip weakening as she shoved against the floor with her legs, arms and back recoiling and bursting outward in an explosive surge that sent a wild stab of pain through his shoulders, his numb, unfeeling arm his only tenuous resistance to death.

His foot found the brake pedal, the car weaving down the center of the highway, then turning on to the gravel as headlights appeared around the curve ahead and roared past, with only the roar of an unmuffled exhaust fading in the darkness and suddenly total exhaustion overwhelmed him, strength vanished as he pressed against the brake, trembling with fatigue, the car stopping short of the barrier of pine as Helen jumped free, tumbling across the gravel, rolling from the car into a drainage ditch that separated the road from the forest. Unhurt, her dress torn, she turned and ran into the woods, a terror-stricken animal seeking refuge in the night.

His head slumped against the wheel, enormous sobs convulsing his chest, eyes blinded by tears. He listened a moment to the idling engine, reached out to turn off the ignition. He heard the whistle of the mainland ferry as another car roared past emerging out of the darkness, racing fingers of light approaching in a crescendo of heavy-throated exhaust that rounded the curve to disappear into the mist. He stared at the open door thinking well, that's that. That's a stupid way to die, and then cold, sour fear stabbed his gut filling his throat with a familiar taste, an old acquaintance returning to remind him that he had been through this before in other shapes and forms and yes this certainly was a stupid way to die. He had seen flaming death, aluminum jack-knifed into twisted pyres of metal and he had seen spiraling corkscrews of trailing smoke plunging towards the sea in almost perfect patterns that instantly vanished on impact, and he had seen planes disintegrate in mid-air, thrown outward in hot fragments that moved away from the center of the explosion so quickly you could fly through the wreckage, and yes, this certainly was no way to die, no way.

He stepped out of the car, the air fresh and moist as the sky cleared, and in the bay other cars crowded the ferry dock, moving slowly towards the loading ramp. He walked into the forest and the fear and taste of death subsided as the scent of pine and the dark rows of trees filled with shadows and mysteries and haunting beauty that called to him. He paused, eyes searching the night, but there was no sign of Helen, no sound or trail beckoning as he entered the forest. He treaded softly on the bed of pine and heard no sound other than his breathing, the stars disappearing, blotted-out by the overhanging branches that enclosed his path as he walked slowly, shuffling his feet on the carpet of cones and pine needles, pausing to listen, turning his head at each reflection, each change in the density of the surrounding blackness.

Somewhere, in this darkness, Helen ran through this forest and he walked carefully, groping, arm extended, his breathing calm, listening to the distant hum of traffic, searching for a sound or movement silhouetted against the sky in the openings between the trees as he raised his eyes searching for a point of light that was a star seen through swaying tree tops. He lost all sense of direction aware of his own breathing, listening to the movement of the pine branches overhead, and his fear was now gone replaced by a feeling of awe and wonder he had experienced many times before.

Alone, at night, flying over the sea he would gaze at the horizon, at the hemisphere of stars slowly rotating through the sky, while below, long phosphorescent rows of wind-driven waves traced white streaks of foam in parallel patterns formed by currents coursing thousands of miles from distant storms. Colliding air masses rising and spinning around each other flowed outward over the sea as mountainous waves tumbled into deep troughs in a continuous movement of power and majesty traversed by the wake of a ship, the stars tracing orderly patterns in a constantly turning arc that enveloped him with only the roar of an engine, the dull, red glow of the instrument panel, the feel of the controls vibrating in his hands providing consciousness of time and place. All sense of here and now vanished and it was the stars that contained his destination, his purpose, the second hand sweeping the face of the chronometer computing an intercept point far above the sea, as he adjusted the trim tabs, his eyes flicking over the instruments as he looked beyond the configurations of the familiar constellations. He flew formation on the universe. His wingman was Orion. And just ahead old Arcturus would lead him in a giant arc to the Big Dipper. Where ever he looked, there was pattern, order. Since the beginning of time.

He felt himself lifted up, transported, a part of this vastness as he looked down at the chartboard on his lap, returning to the course line and checkpoint, the time, the heading, the speed that were tenuous links with a moving flight deck somewhere below. Yes, out there, beyond him, were concepts of time and space vaguely perceived, and the mystery of it all overwhelmed him. Yes, there is meaning. Yes, there is God. But how does one tell, how does one explain the importance of convoys steaming through this night, the task forces and escort ships weaving patterns of attack and defense across an indifferent sea? How does one tell? Flying under the stars these feelings seemed right and true and filled with promise of a future that could only be glimpsed as a tentative hope, a vague impulse, a hunger for life. How does one hold on to this need within oneself? Bringing it all to flower? The answer could be found among the stars and flying between sky and sea, hour after hour, the monotony of each patrol was filled with feelings that grew more intense each night.

And now she nearly killed him.

In the dark woods he reached out and touched a tree, a flood of feeling calmed him, his trembling ceased as the silence of the forest, the scent of pitch filled the night, strangely comforting him, transforming terror and exhaustion into tranquil peace. He felt weak, his legs folding under him as he sat sprawling under the canopy of pine. He laid his head down on his arm, and in a moment was asleep.

FIVE

She heard the car on the gravel drive, the low rumble of a garage door opening, and then the irritating sound of keys fumbling in the lock. Always fumbling with his goddamn keys. A clumsy man. He entered through the kitchen as she picked up a book and pretended to read as if this was how she passed the day.

"Hello," he said, his face flushed from the cold, one hand raised in a "thumbs-up" salute so familiar to warriors.

"I made it," he said. "A hell-of-a drive." She turned and looked over her shoulder as he sprawled into the arm-chair, a mess of rumpled clothes and uncombed hair.

"Good book?" he asked.

"I don't know, yet."

"Remind me never to drive home from the city on a Friday," he said. "I'm shell-shocked."

"Traffic bad?"

"Worse than bad. Don't see how any civilized human being can commute day after day." He leaned back and closed his eyes, the lines of his face softened into a shapeless blur half-hidden in the shadows.

"Tired?"

"Exhausted."

She watched his head fall back against the chair. In a moment he would be asleep. Instant, child-like sleep. No tossing. No turning. No torment. Positively inhuman.

"Let's go out to dinner?" she asked.

"OK"

"Steve?'

"Yes?'

"Wake in half an hour?"

"That's all I need."

The room was Rembrandt. Dark shadows. Behind him, the window admitted the sun's afterglow. She loved this time of day. Soon the room would be dark, and she tucked the blanket around her neck. She looked up and fixed her eyes on cracks in the ceiling. Cracks would be where the bugs come from. If ever there were bugs. Someday, they say, bugs will come crawling all over you, but of course that's later. There's always bugs crawling in movies, and you writhe on the floor with imaginary insects crawling all over you and you scream, My God how you scream like Ray Milland before he lost his hair. How terrible not to wear a hairpiece. He was so handsome. How sad, to lose your beauty. He wasn't acting, he was so real fighting those bugs but then again, Isadora Duncan was superb, the way she tossed that long red scarf over her shoulder in that cute little Bugatti roadster. She never hallucinated. No, thank God. Just a long scarf wrapped around the hub of a wheel. God, how superb! After all that drinking and dancing, and that terrible Russian lover, that horrible poet. Of course she did drink a lot. Bette Davis, in Dark Victory died well. Great acting.

They never die that way in real life. Never. Not even Bette Davis popping her eyes out can die like the real thing. There's no harsh rattling sounds and a pitiful voice pleading because what people say when they are dying is not nice. Funerals are easy compared to dying when the screaming begins. "I don't want to die! I don't want to die! I don't want to die!" It goes on and on and on like the time listening outside a bedroom door she heard a voice calling, and through the crack in the door she watched a fist pounding the wall, each blow ebbing a life away as if warding-off death by striking plaster, the thump, thump, thump of a fist growing weaker, the intervals between blows lengthening until the thumping was inaudible and she saw that even after death that thin arm reflexively beating a fist against the wall. The voice silent. The fist now striking air, the tubes connected to inverted flasks suspended above the bed until the arm dropped, the needle taped into the vein, the fist, that defiant fist, still clenched in final, irrevocable death.

"Goodbye World!"

"What did you say, Helen?"

"Nothing. Just talking." She watched him shift in his chair. A dark, ominous form, vaguely threatening.

"Aren't you going to turn on the lights?"

"Letting you sleep. You look peaceful, sleeping."

He grunted. "I thought we were going out to dinner?"

"In a while. In a little while," she said. Dining-out was her passion. It did not matter where. Dining-out sounded elegant. No matter how noisy or crowded, no matter how bad the service, dining-out was their catechism, a parade of expensive menus, French, Italian, Greek, Russian, Spanish; and exotic salads tossed and served, the waiter bringing silver ice buckets for champagne and when there was candlelight she was happy, a child on Christmas morning. Yes, going out to dinner was a joy.

"I think I'll wash," he said, rising from the chair, and she closed her eyes and listened as he climbed the stairs, each step pounding the wood. The slam of the bathroom door jangled her nerves but she grew calm as she imagined him scraping his wiry stubble. In a direct light, he always needed a shave and thank God he was aware of it. She switched on the reading light as he walked down stairs.

"How do I look?" he asked, smiling, hat in hand. A beggar soliciting praise.

"Just fine. Fine. I'll be with you in a minute," she said.

In the bathroom she wiped steam off the mirror. Yes, she did have a good face, high cheekbones puffed-out with flesh. Interesting eyes. It was her smile that won the day. Her smile. Worked wonders, thank God. Of course everything else could fade away but her smile would always carry her past the point of no return for beauty. Having small eyes, a great asset. No one ever saw what you thought. So, if she attracted men with her eyes, she won them with her smile, and it all started early.

The mirror was full-length in the hallway of her parent's home, and she admired herself in a skirt with a starched apron and puffed sleeves covering her thin arms. A tenth birthday gift. There in front of the mirror she had her first sight of the woman she would someday be. A cap completed the costume.

She placed it on her head, turning in the mirror as she set the pins. She studied her image and when she turned from the mirror she saw the chauffeur smiling at her. "Oh Miss Helen, how beautiful you are!"

He was enthralled, truly enthralled, and she had never seen this look of adoration before. Without a word, he opened his arms and she leapt into his embrace. "Happy birthday, Miss Helen, happy birthday!" he said, kissing her on the cheek, and she felt his chest heave as he held her in his arms, his eyes crinkly as he spun her around, doing a pirouette, his thick arms enveloping her as a wave of emotion spread through her arms out to her fingertips as she arched her back, pressing herself against him, the colors in the room turning gold and red and orange as an unfamiliar convulsion shuddered inside her, and she was oh so happy, so filled with joy, breathless, as wave after wave of feeling subsided and she became calm as he released her from his embrace, and she stared up at him with wonder, he smiling that same smile of adoration as she felt these strange feelings diminish and her calm became exhaustion, a weariness so complete she stared at the floor as she walked out of the room.

That night, in bed, a pillow under her head, she felt his arms around her, once again felt his dizzying pirouette as he spun her around and around, his head thrown back, the crinkles in his eyes laughing as he embraced her and she arched back pressing herself towards the ceiling, her face and throat tense, her fists clenched, her legs rigid as the colors on the ceiling became orange and red and gold and her eyelids fluttered concentrating all her strength as a sudden convulsive wave of feeling exploded again and again, tremors of sensation flooding her body as she fell back limp, opening her eyes, watching the colors change as her arms and legs and groin were bathed in a warmth she found delicious. Again and again she arched her back, grew tense, closed her eyes, and concentrated on creating this delicious warmth, these waves of feeling that left her exhausted and happy.

Never again did she allow the chauffeur to do more than open a door for her, and she looked forward to each night when she entered a strange and wonderful world of sensations, the cold feel of the sheet, the rough texture of the blanket, the dark shadows, inflaming her mind, for on the ceiling appeared an endless parade of fantastic shapes and colors creating a fever of emotion, an eruption of images that exploded each night when she closed her eyes.

Downstairs, Steve was stirring a drink as she entered the room and he saluted her with his glass. "Just a weak scotch," he explained. "That's all."

"We'll be late." She stared at the drink in his hand. "Our reservation is eight-thirty."

At the restaurant they sat at a corner table, the candlelight flickering under low, wooden beams. The waiter, pencil in hand, stared down at his parishioners.

"Two martinis, please. Tell the bartender they're for the Irwins."

The waiter vanished. "I love their martinis," she said turning to Steve. The candlelight softened his features. He looked younger. But still, she had never seen anyone sit a chair that way. So relaxed. A big lump of flesh. Not a nerve. Not a single, Goddamn nerve in his body.

"Just one drink, OK?"

"Right."

The waiter placed an oversized glass on the table and she studied the clear liquid precisely contained in the inverted, chilled cone that felt so alive in her hand. She raised her glass.

"Cheers."

"Cheers."

Just like professor Pavlov's dogs. Cheers. Chin Chin! Prost. Sante. Le Chaim. Bottoms Up. Down the Hatch. Up Yours. Sempre Duro. Svoboda. Sayonara. She sipped her drink. Not bad. Pavlov's canines never had it so good. Only after telling someone you love them, one thousand times, it does become reflexive when you program your soul with words you don't feel. I love you repeated oh so many times becomes as meaningless as raising a glass.

"How's your drink?"

"How's yours?"

"Fine."

"They do make a terrific martini, don't they?"

"Yes."

She remembered when she woke one morning and realized she loved the son of a bitch. No. That's not true. He's not a son of a bitch. It's just that he drives her up the wall. Driving her to drink. Idiot writers, nibbling away, day after day, page by page, solemn drudges chewing at their vanities, spewing out their plays and books. She told him that she loved him and she did mean it, and besides it was about time she had a husband, being a wife wasn't exactly a prison sentence, and although no man could compete with her fantasies in bed, the sex wasn't bad. All in all, it wasn't a rotten deal if only she could keep the drinking under control. And besides, he adored her.

He truly loved her. Made her feel loved. There was no doubt about that. If only he could learn to sit like something human.

"Would you care for the menu?"

"Not yet. Please. Let's not rush. Let's take our time. I'm enjoying myself."

"I'm starved."

"All right," she said. "Order now. But ask them not to rush. I'm having another."

"How about wine?"

"Whatever you say."

She'd been good all day. She felt pleased. She really was on top of her drinking. Yes, waiting for his goddamn telephone calls, her daily life tyrannized by a bell. That's when the drinking started. Dear Professor Pavlov! Or is it Professor Love? The bell rang and I couldn't stop salivating. The sound of his footsteps, his voice, and even the smell of his hair tonic and I became damp! No wonder my drinking got out of control.

"Marriage didn't solve a thing."

"What did you say?"

"I said marriage didn't solve a thing."

"I don't understand."

"I know," she said. "Neither do I."

She felt flushed. Leaned back in her chair, fighting tension.

"What are you staring at?"

"Shadows."

He turned and looked over his shoulder.

"What do you see?"

"Shadows."

"No elephants?"

"That's not funny."

"I'm sorry."

"The hell with your sorry."

"Helen. Are you all right?"

She nodded.

"Let's forget about the wine.?"

"OK"

"Good."

Right. One's the limit tonight. One. The most important word of all. One nation, One world. One God. One drink. One husband. One life. One mother. One father. One chance. Just one. One truth. Yes, it's all in the words. It's all in the words. And finally, there is only one word and that word is love.

"He's waiting for your order, Helen."

"I'm not hungry."

"Eat something, please."

She looked up at the waiter. His face was beautiful. A real smile. Not one of those synthetic restaurant grins that kills appetite. She never looked at waiters. "I'll have fish," she said.

"Excellent choice, Madame."

Excellent choice indeed! God! Such life and death decisions. She loved fish.

"Would you like coffee with your meal, dear?"

"A barbaric thought," she said. "Civilized people have wine with their meals."

"I know."

She was feeling fine. By the time food arrived, she would be hungry. Steve was leaning forward in his chair, looking around the room. Observing. Always observing. At the corner table a red-faced woman chewed with grinding jaws, her husband thrust chunks of meat into a small mouth, their children bent over their plates, gorging themselves. At the next table an elegant old couple delicately lifted their food, invisibly chewing between tightly pressed lips, and how touching, the way he poured wine into her glass. Yes, graciousness. You didn't see that anymore. The way he turned the neck of the bottle, pouring half a glass without spilling a drop. Her father could do that. Her father did everything elegantly. An instinctive gentleman. Not a single detail of his life lacked style. A vanishing breed, gracious men. Oh, how she missed him.

A large party circled a nearby table and came to rest. She waited for Steve to react. But where was he? Writing in his head? That vague look. His other life. His other wife. He was here and yet he was not here. His hours of inaccessible confinement a crashing bore. His joyous solitude was her loneliness. He was a sleepwalker. A Zombie. A Golem. He could sit through dinner without saying a word as she conducted a monologue. He would nod, and at intervals, comment, but there never was another half to a conversation. His half remained in his head, unstated, and yes, he did enjoy listening to her. Day after day he slipped off into his other world. He wasn't a person. He was a word machine. And for a while, a pretty good fucking machine. Lord high deliverer of that holy of holies, the orgasm. As a companion he was an absolute zero. Jesus Christ himself could sit at the next table and he wouldn't look up from his thoughts.

The waiter placed a dish before her and she looked at him and smiled.

"Anything else, madam?"

"No thank you."

"Sir?" he turned to Steve.

"No thank you."

Again she smiled at the waiter. He looked at her acknowledging a gesture beyond courtesy.

"Notice something about that waiter?" she asked.

"No."

"You're a writer. Didn't you see anything at all?"

"I didn't give him a thought."

"You missed something important."

"I can't see everything."

"He was afraid."

"He looked happy."

"I know fear when I see it."

"He was smiling."

"Everybody smiles. It means nothing. God! Can't you judge people by more than a surface appearance?"

"It's a waiter's job to smile. It comes with the black tie."

"It's in his eyes. Fear! He's a refugee. Hungarian. His age would be just right."

"Right for what?"

"To be Hungarian. 1956 was the uprising. That's when he escaped."

"How do you know that?"

"His fading accent."

"I liked his accent."

"He did everything but kiss my hand. He was gallant."

"You were flirting."

"I smiled."

"Well?"

"One lonely human being to another."

"Woman to man you mean."

"That's a pathetic Boy Scout point of view."

"Let's drop the subject."

"I know about fear," she said. "People live all

their lives afraid. Afraid of parents, police, afraid of losing a job, getting sick, growing old, dying. People who don't have a fear in their body don't understand being afraid."

"It's never as bad as all that."

"Look around this room. For one brief moment we huddle together and eat and drink and share a little animal warmth so as to not be afraid. Fear, not love is the first truly profound emotion we are aware of. The first taste we remember is the taste of fear and in childhood you have butterflies in your gut that made you wet your pants. There was more fear walking to school than in going to war. God gave us weakness and hatred and envy and cruelty. Those are God's gifts. He gave us imagination to intensify the terror in every shadow, every closet, every unlighted attic transformed by a child's imagination into a chamber of horrors. And each night, we are condemned to fear, comforted by a good-night kiss, and there you lay in darkness with every sound, every squeak, every shape evoking terror. Those are our first lessons. Paternal love won't wipe out the memory of that howling, squalling rage at being alone and afraid. Illusions of human goodness are nonsense. Depravity, decadence, corruption are the true character of life and only a fool thinks otherwise. God in his infinite wisdom gives us blindness so we never see Evil except occasionally on the seven o'clock news. We have blood on our hands because evil is the reality we live by. So if you love life, you better accept that you are in love with evil for that is what life truly is. Evil!"

She stared at him, choking back emotions evoked by her words. She looked around the room. The other guests stared down at their food refusing to meet the challenge of her eyes.

"You were shouting."

She was annoyed at his calm smile. "You weren't listening."

"Everyone heard you."

She shook her head. "You're hopeless. You really are hopeless. Don't you have anything to say?"

"To what?"

"To what I said."

"There's no answer. I don't agree, that's all. And if I tell you why, we'll fight. This is the last decent restaurant we are not too embarrassed to enter."

"That's a goddamn lie!"

"Well, I'm embarrassed."

"I don't want to fight."

"Neither do I."

She neatly sliced her food, spearing a piece of fish with her fork. She was shouting. She could see it on all the faces. Was it smugness or greed that produced that look? How superior they felt. Yes, she had made another scene. The Hungarian with his charming manner was shocked. Well, that's me, all right. The me of me!

"Care for desert?"

"What's the rush?"

"There's none. Just thought I'd order something sweet."

She shook her head. Yes, the waiter was smiling. He was listening. Europeans have a great sense of life's tragedy. They know all about evil. Especially Hungarians. Goodness, truth, and beauty. What crap! That's all you know and all you need to know. Only little David could stop big Goliath with a stone. A fairy tale. The meek shall inherit disaster! And if she can make it through this meal she will have earned that big drink waiting for her at home.

"Coffee?"

"Yes, please."

As they sipped coffee she stepped back in her mind observing their dining ritual. The restaurant was a temple. The candles burnt offerings. The tables, altars where worshippers sliced and stabbed and chewed their way to paradise or was it an early grave? The thick gravies, the fatty meats, the whipped cream on the fudge cake, and the delicious wine. The drinks, the drinks, the drinks and then the check please. Thank you very much.

"What did you say?"

"I said thank you very much."

"You were mumbling."

Amazing how strong one drink can be. Was her speech clear? And how many ounces of alcohol destroy how many brain cells? She could not recall. A profound insult to the brain doctors were fond of saying.

"To hell with it."

"The hell with what?"

"Evil."

"What do you mean?"

"I love it. I just love it. I love Evil," she said.

SIX

Tonight was not a night for sleep. He stared out the window watching moonlight print stark branches of leafless trees against the sky, intricate silhouettes with multiple arms rising from snow-covered earth. His brain was agitated. He studied the lights on the far shore tracing a narrow highway thru the hills. Over the hills and through the woods. He smiled. To grandfather's house we go was the next line. The horse knows the way, to carry the sleigh, through the white and frosted snow. His mother sang that. High overhead, jets converged on New York and he watched frozen contrails disperse ice crystals, millions of minute reflectors sending moonlight back to earth. Mother moon. Father sun. Their child is earth, for earth is human. He turned away from the window, away from his sleeping wife. Great God almighty! Peace at last! He walked downstairs. He was set for another performance of Soldiers of Despair, marching and counter-marching through the long dark night of my soul. The longest running show in memory. Act One: I am born. Act Two: I suffer. Act Three: I die. All my chickens come home to roost.

He crossed the living room to the window facing the water. The huge bulk of a ship rounded the point where the river emerges from between the narrow highlands. He listened to the throb of diesel engines and watched the wake of the ship, the energy imparted by the moving hull rebounding from the riverbank to create a counter-wave. He put on a heavy parka. The path down to the dock was steep, and he dug his heels into the snow with each step. The air was cold, and when he looked back at the house the white walls glowed in reflected moonlight. At the dock he reached under the overturned dinghy to pull out the oars, sweeping snow off the hull with the blades. Grasping the gunwale he turned it right side up. Dragging the boat to the edge of the dock, he slid it into the river.

It felt good to again hold oars in his hands, the wood hard and true. Digging the blades into the water the boat glided ahead with each stroke. He reached out, arms extended, dipping the blades down as he swung at the hips, pushing against the stern of the dinghy with his feet, each powerful stroke lifting and driving the boat forward. He steered by a straight wake trailing after him, his blades tracing a path across the water. He shifted weight altering the balance of the boat, his easy rhythm conserving strength, the power of his shoulders flowing through his arms, through the oars and into the water. He could see home, a spectral glow on the distant shore. A high layer of stratus clouds covered the moon darkening trees, dulling the snow-covered slope. His breathing relaxed, and under the parka he felt sweat plastering his shirt to his skin. The tide began to ebb strengthening the downstream current.

He rested on the oars, raising the blades, gliding

through the water, listening to the hiss of bubbles under the stern. His mind was clear and sharp like the night. Yes, he still loved her. There was no doubt about that. But they both were in danger, real danger. The Law of Inevitable Consequences. She was programmed for death. Fascinated by death. She had a hunger for destruction. And there wasn't a damn thing he could do to stop her. He felt fury rising and he grabbed the oars and rowed towards the deepwater channel marked by blinking lights. He was being manipulated. An accomplice. She was on railroad tracks and she didn't want a change in destination.

The dinghy glided ahead, the rhythm of his rowing slowed as he prolonged the recovery of each stroke, his breath steaming as he exhaled. "Accomplice! My name is Accomplice!" he shouted. "God damn it to hell, anyway!" He pulled hard, once, twice, three times, and then rested, sliding the oars across his lap, the dinghy rocking gently as he shifted in the seat, turning to look over his shoulder at the blinking lights marking the channel. The ebb tide set with increasing strength, the current drifting him to the edge of safety.

He looked downriver. Lights outlined the bridge extending from the foot of a mountain at a wide sweeping curve in the valley. On the horizon, forty miles away, the glow of the city washed-out the stars. He turned to look at the northern sky as a shower of stars burned a fiery trail across the heavens. He was on railroad tracks too. There was no doubt about that. And he didn't like the destination. He wanted out! Well then, what was there to stop him? Love? Duty? Responsibility? Bullshit? He was still riding that train, one hand on the throttle, one hand on the brake because he wanted to. He was still here because he was here, because he was here, and only he could do a damn thing about it. There was no lock on the door. He could always leave, if he really wanted to.

He tightened the drawstrings on the hood of his parka. Yes, of all the things he had loved, this world of stars and sea had never once broken his heart. Never once let him down. He loved this one thing that could never return his love anymore than a page of printed prose upon which he lavished so much devotion could return love.

Gentlemen of the jury, examine the evidence. The great Law of Inevitable Consequences is clear. I make no plea of innocence. I am both victim and perpetrator. True, I didn't throw the cigarette butts into the waste paper basket but neither did I empty that basket before retiring. Neither did I close the window behind the stove thus allowing the wind to blow out the flame left burning, as were the cigarettes in question by a somewhat inebriated wife. Saved by a nose, your honor, for the odor of gas and smoke are quite distinct, and so the defendant mounted his white horse instead of his wife saving her life instead of implanting his precious seed. The defense rests.

No touch of wind stirred the water, and his movements gently rocked the dinghy. The tide accelerated the current ebbing out to sea. A distant lighthouse blinked one long flash, followed by two short flashes to mark the bend in the river where the mountains formed a narrow gorge. Slowly he began counting the rhythmic flashes of light, and in a moment, was asleep.

A strange sleep. He imagined he heard the first sharp crack of a starting cartridge spinning the propellers of an aircraft, sucking fuel into the cylinders, bringing the engine alive with a stuttering roar that rose to a crescendo as the blades changed pitch, their whirling tips attacking the air at a new angle, the sound rising and falling from a whine to a low-throated roar of harnessed power. Then he heard this sound fade leaving only the wavering notes of unsynchronized engines flying high overhead, their throbbing beat tracing a path across the sky. Then he heard emerging from the distance, a single low pulsing throb, a beat of energy traveling across the water slowly increasing in intensity, the rhythmic pounding of pistons growing louder until he heard the solid thrashing of a ship's propellers slicing down into the water, turning slowly as they approached and then he heard the bells of an engine-room telegraph answering a signal from the bridge, the sharp shrill sound of a bosun's whistle crackling over a loudspeaker as he opened his eyes and looked up at a solid wall of steel moving directly at him, the bow wave flaring out to either side of a ship as he read the markings painted on a hull covered with red-leaded patches of rust, masthead lights towering overhead, feeling the dinghy rise under him with the advancing wave that spun him around as he pulled back on the oars. He heard the engines pounding, the water rushing past the hull, the wave rising higher and higher spinning the dinghy as he dug the blades deep into the white froth tumbling over and over as the huge bulk of the ship shouldered its way downriver. Then he felt the suction of the wake pull the dinghy against the steel plates, one oar wedged between the gunwales breaking, the oarlock scraping a jagged scar in the brown rust at the waterline, the dinghy crashing in against the ship as he heard the slashing propellers, the giant blades turning under the hull, whirlpools of spinning turbulence roiling the surface, overturning the dinghy, pulling him down into the maelstrom, down into the dark spinning void that rolled him over and over, his arms wildly thrashing, his lungs gasping mouthfuls of water, convulsively retching, burning stabs of pain inflaming his chest as he heaved out his guts in one long spasm of fear.

The air trapped inside his parka carried him to the surface tumbling in the swirling waters of the wake. He felt the turbulence decrease and he reached out grasping the gunwale of the dinghy. He coughed his lungs clear, his vision going red with each spasmodic effort to expel brackish salt water. He rested, watching the stern lights of the ship disappear and then he pressed down, submerging the near side of the dinghy, pulling the opposite gunwale towards him, righting the swamped boat floating awash in the fast-moving current. He moved to the stern, pushing down, rocking the craft fore and aft, sloshing out the water, the dinghy floating higher until desperately, he pulled himself up into the boat.

Using both hands he bailed, working slowly, the precarious balance of the boat returning. "God!" he said to himself. "My God!" and then he began trembling, shivers of cold fear ran up his back, his arms and hands shaking violently. Yes, he was alive, the stars were overhead, and he could still feel the vibrations of propellers and swirling waters and his mouth tasted of oil and brown river scum and the presence of death.

The wake of the ship became a flat trail of bubbles floating down the channel and the first return of the bow wave rebounding from shore gently rocked the dinghy. The current flowed towards the outside bend in the river where the dredged channel crossed to the opposite bank to pass between supporting towers of the bridge. The dinghy floated broadside to the current, drifting towards an island of ice-covered rocks and a channel marker and he stared at the light. He felt cold and removed his parka, wringing out the water. Quickly dressing, he shivered as the wet cloth pressed against his skin. He felt the dinghy drift against the rocks and he reached out to tie a line around a stone jutting from the island and he saw his one unbroken oar wedged between slabs of ice. Struggling to his feet he began climbing, wedging his boots in the crevices, forcing his fingers into the cracks. Warmed by the effort, anticipating safety at the base of that steel tower he wedged the side of his hand between two rocks, swinging his foot up in search of the next higher ledge, groping to find a platform of ice-covered rock, sliding his foot onto it, arms and back straining as he raised himself over the granite shoving down hard with his legs, lunging on to the island. He closed his eyes, blinded by the flashing light, and when he opened them he sat there alone. A solitary survivor of disaster.

SEVEN

The images on the screen merged, the women reached out to each other, their eyes illuminated with the joy of mutual discovery as their hands caressed the contours of their bodies. They embraced, coming together as if exploring a miracle. There were no words. Laughter and sighs and eloquent silence were their only language.

Helen Irwin watched the film, possessed by sadness. As one woman began crying, Helen felt the convulsive thrust of a sob rising from her anguish as she clutched the arm of the seat.

Then seated in front of her a man stared back over his shoulder diverting her from the screen. She concentrated on the film, aware of being watched as the performers consoled one another. Then she saw a bulky shadow move towards the aisle as the images behind it embraced and a calm enveloped Helen as a stranger side-stepped a row of seats and sat beside her. On the screen one woman bared her breast to her lover who laid her head on this lovely white bosom. Helen watched hoping for that burst of emotion that was catharsis, the ultimate release towards which this film had been progressing and then she felt a hand on her arm and she pulled away, rising to her feet, moving along the row of seats towards the aisle, fury blinding her as she hurried towards the door.

In the lobby she waited for her eyes to adjust to the light, putting on dark glasses she fled the theater. Diesel fumes and a jostling throng closed in upon her as she walked to the street, the crowd coiling about her, nameless people peering out of cold eyes and lifeless faces pushing and shoving as she struggled to walk, and now, the ultimate indignity, she could no longer sit in a theater alone, unmolested. There would always be a shadow emerging from the darkness and with a word, a clearing of a throat, a touch of a hand, disturb her fixation on the screen, shattering concentration with unwelcome advances. Disgusting. She adored movies. And now this solace was denied her by the sick imaginings of God knows what kind of men seeking to exploit loneliness. There was something pure about sitting in the dark, with even the most intimate companion unwanted. She preferred to sit alone, and now, that pleasure was impossible.

She looked across the street and saw a tricolor awning extending over scrubbed wooden tables. The entrance of a restaurant. She entered a dimly lit room. The maitre d' escorted her to a table, offering her a menu.

"Just a Martini," she said. "Very dry, s'il vous plait."

The waiter nodded, and stepped to the bar. She studied the murals on the wall. Sunny France? No. That's Italy. Sunny Italy. France is what? She glanced down at the matches in the ashtray. Why of course. La Belle France! Beautiful France. Not a bad name for a restaurant. She recalled the movie, the flow of images unreeling echoes of memory and in a moment she was suffused with feeling. The death scene was fantastic. The way that woman died. And the little girl in the white dress! The long gloves were right. Absolutely right. Every detail perfection. That's how she felt once upon a time. That's what wearing a white dress made her feel, but of course all that changed. It always changes.

The waiter served the drink. She felt fury dissolve as she sipped slowly, her knot of anger unlocking when she noticed the telephone on the wall. She opened her purse, probing for a coin. Yes, that was a brilliant idea. It was just what he needed. She dialed the operator and then listened to the ringing of the phone.

"Steve?" she said. "I missed the express. I am at a cute little place called La Bell France."

"Where?"

"It's in the book, I'm sure."

She glanced at the clock. Almost Six. He certainly would be finished working. "Yes," she said, "I'm sure you'd enjoy this place. The Menu looks inviting, and the prices are ridiculous."

"I couldn't make it in less than an hour. Hour and a half."

"That's all right. Take your time."

She returned to her seat. The adjacent table now occupied. These goddamn cheek-by-jowl restaurants. A big empty room and they seat customers side by side. No fair. All she wanted was to sit alone. Relax. And now she had this stranger to contend with. Well, she wasn't going to look at him. No! She sipped her drink, luxuriating in its effect, leaning back in her chair to study the harvest scene on the wall. A row of peasants, scythes in hand, stooping to the earth, gleaning. The gleaners. Yes. The gleaners. By Millet. Not Edna St. Vincent, but the painter. The sky marvelous. The horizon low, and the cloud streaks gave the figures a religious glow. There was a spiritual quality to the light. The mural was alive. She closed her eyes, squinting, and the stooped figures became silhouettes. The sky darkened. The gleaners now menacing, their hands digging into the ground as if plundering the earth. She opened her eyes and smiled. Magic! Just a matter of how you looked at the world.

She signaled the waiter who brought another drink. The maitre d' escorted two couples to a table under the mural. Expensively gowned women, and men, she observed, not worth a glance. Beefy, gray, watery flesh, two gobs of mashed potatoes with something obscene where eyes and mouths should be. Handsomely dressed without an attractive smile in the group. She raised her drink. This would be her last. She would definitely stop at two. She was in control. Shrill voices, laughter, filled the room. Damn. Just when she was feeling great. Enjoying herself.

"I agree with you," the man at the adjacent table said. She stared at him. He was smiling, a thin cigar poised between manicured fingers. "Finding a quiet place to drink is impossible."

She frowned. He wore a ring on one finger. "I detest the odor of cigars," she said. Yes the ring was too large. Vulgar. And his hands were too small for a man.

"I beg your pardon," he said, jabbing the stub into the ash tray.

She turned and stared at the mural. She could feel the man glowering. The fading trace of smoke spiraled-up from the ash tray. The mood was wrong. Just like in the theater. Some bastard always comes along and spoils everything.

The man stared at her. She could feel his eyes pressing against the back of her neck. A mood of disquiet came over her, a familiar feeling, a feeling of helplessness, the eternal victim doomed to live her life threatened by the boorish, the insensitive, the callous, and the cruel. There was nothing so vulgar as unwanted attention and she could not walk down a street, watch a movie, or have a drink by herself without being victimized. Yes, it was her nightmare. Helen's horror. She did nothing to attract attention. Nothing. She wore her most conservative dress. More like a schoolgirl with a single strand of pearls at her neck than a mature woman. Yet there was no respite, no escape from this torment. No matter where, no matter when, no matter how discrete or aloof her behavior, they stared, they grimaced, they touched her arms, her breast, she could no longer ride a bus, a subway, a crowded elevator. Yes, it was horrible. She could not feel safe in a cab, leaning back in her seat, alone, enjoying the privacy of the moment, seeing in the rear-view mirror the driver staring, that lascivious look, the overt lust, as if every man wanted to fuck her. Sweet Jesus! What a world. Those two eyes were boring holes in her neck. She nodded at the maitre d' who came to her table.

"I'm expecting my husband," she said. The maitre d' smiled and turned to escort a young couple to a table. There is nothing so disturbing as a woman alone. And that was her problem. She enjoyed being alone. Preferred being alone to enduring the company of almost anyone she could think of. God! What a world. What bastards. They want you living their little lives, thinking their pukey thoughts, trapped in their pathetic emotions and when you are one of them they shit all over you. Rape of the body is absolutely antiseptic compared to what most people will do to your soul given half a chance. She was warm and gracious and most people are terrified of such a person. They're suspicious. They think you want something from them. God damn right! I want courtesy. Consideration. Good manners. Is that too much to ask?

She listened to him order his meal, selecting carefully, discussing each item in a cultivated voice. A nice voice. Almost elegant. An actor? A UN delegate? Possibilities unlimited. Perhaps a gentleman? You can tell a lot about people by the way they speak. Still, she was troubled by his voice. It certainly wasn't a boarding school voice. Or American. More like BBC out of London's East End. God! The hybrid voices you hear. The TV announcers shall not inherit our ears, dear God. There'd be no living with those booming bassos reverberating from coast to coast. Her fingers fumbled open a package of cigarettes and placed one between her lips. A gold lighter appeared instantly and she leaned towards the flame, inhaling, nodding thanks to the stranger. The mating dance. First, the unlit cigarette. Then, male to the rescue. Next move to the female. Dropping a handkerchief is only good for openers. She could continue to ignore him. But then she'd be rude, wouldn't she?

"Waiting for someone?"

"My husband."

"I hope he does not disappoint you."

"He never does."

Her tone was right. She felt proud of herself. Polite. Well-bred. Not encouraging. He was of course, an actor. His voice reeked vanity. "Waiting for someone?" What the hell did he think she was doing here? Trying to pick him up? What an ass. Still he was attractive. Well-dressed. But that voice. That damn phony arty-farty theatrical voice out of Uta Hagen by Lee Strasberg by the Actor's Studio by for all she knew out of Brooklyn or the Bronx. He was elegant as a prince. Yes. That was who he reminded her of. That prince married to that skinny washed-out blond from Philadelphia. Telling a prince from a pauper was quite a problem. His voice went right through her. Her first instinct was to curtsy. A real aristocratic put-down kind of voice that had just the right tone of arrogance. Her voice lacked arrogance. Her voice was too warm. Too inviting. It created problems. Even the fat butcher at the supermarket misinterpreted her tone. She tried to be nice to everyone. But if you're nice you get hurt. Being too nice doesn't pay. A superior, aristocratic, arrogant voice saves you a lot of problems. People keep their distance. No question in anyone's mind that your body and soul are forbidden territory.

"May I buy you a drink?"

She stared at him, hesitating. "Thank you," she said as he signaled the waiter who glided to their table, eyebrows raised.

"I believe a martini? Extra dry," he said. The waiter nodded. It would have been rude to refuse, she told herself, smiling.

"Don't think I make a habit of this sort of thing," he said.

"Nor I," she answered.

God! Bette Davis and guess who? What dialogue!

This one's an original. Everything but a carnation in his button hole. And his cologne would melt the polish off her fingernails. OK Buster. What's next? If you're going to be who you are, than I'm going to be Miss Davis in her greatest role and we'll both do all right as long as we saw the same Late Show and you stayed awake during the big scenes.

"Are you living in New York?"

"No."

"I would have thought you were," he said.

"Why?"

"The way you dress."

"How's that?"

"Only a New Yorker could dress so plainly, simply, and bring such style to what she's wearing."

"Oh My God."

"What's the matter?"

"You're in the dress business."

"How did you know?"

"I know," she said, the romance of the scene crashing, her incentive to play, vanishing. Bette Davis never did a scene with anyone in the dress business. Not on her chinny chin chin she didn't!

"It's my job to notice how women dress."

"Really?"

"Yes. In this room you are the only woman who is not overdressed."

"Thank You."

"Under-dressing is a style, you know. That's how Jackie calls attention to herself."

"How's that?"

"Under-dressing. Simple outfits. Solid colors. Absence of jewelry, you know. That finishing school look in a grown woman. It is most attractive."

"Shit."

"What did you say?"

"You're full of shit."

"I beg your pardon."

"You're full of crap. Overdressing. Underdressing. This look! That look! You don't know a tit from a tiara."

His face flushed. He returned to his food. She had been shouting. The room was silent. She could hear his knife scrape his plate. The maitre d' approached, scowling. Two gobs of mashed potatoes for faces at the next table looked pained. In their open mouths she saw unchewed food between gaping teeth. A Hogarth drawing.

"You've had too much to drink," the man said.

"Right. Absolutely right."

The concerned maitre d' hovered over the table. "Is there something wrong, madam?" he asked. She snubbed her cigarette in the ash tray. What a sweetheart, that maitre d'. He'd fight a duel for her. But how should this scene be played? Tallulah's modulated gentility? Or perhaps a rip-roaring all-stops-out spitfire Bette Davis wearing a flaming red gown speaking for all women who have ever been humiliated.

She sat straight in her chair pushing the drink away. "This gentleman," she said, glancing at the stranger, "Is no gentleman. Please bring my check." She shoved the table, spilling her drink, rising, head high, steadying herself on a chair.

The maitre d' swung the table aside as if opening a gate. "I'm most unhappy," he said. "Please accept our apologies." He scowled at the stranger. Then, whispering. "One is not able to pick and choose customers, you know." His face sagged. "New York has changed." He escorted her to the door as all notice of the incident instantly obliterated in loud talk.

In the street she searched for signal lights on passing cabs but the only fish swimming in this neon sea were off-duty.

She plunged directly into the crowd, the shop windows shading faces a sickly pallor of colorless lips and hollow eyes. She walked through a throng of half-faces feeling contaminated.

A policeman leered at her. She looked at him, uncomprehending as he pointed his nightstick at a theater poster displaying oversized breasts. The cashier huddled in a glass booth, a shabby fur coat held tight around her chest as she slid tickets and change out onto the counter.

"Keep moving, sister," the policeman said. "I'm not going to tell you again."

She stumbled against an unmoving, solid body, its leather coat collar framing an enormous face scowling through pin-pointed eyes that expanded as she stared into their unremitting malignancy.

"Baby!" he said, "I don't know who you are, or who you're working for, but you sure as hell don't belong on my turf!" He smiled, displaying enormous teeth. "Do your trickin' elsewhere. I'm sure you get my meaning!" He vanished into the crowd.

She felt a hand on her arm. The policeman smiled. Apologetic. "I didn't know you were one of his girls," he said laughing. "I'm new around here."

She opened her mouth to speak but only the high-pitched shriek of an ambulance could be heard and she abandoned her effort to explain, to protest, to erase humiliation.

She turned into a side street and paused at a window to study her reflection, the glass creating a parody of her face. "Yes, you are a great beauty," she said aloud, "a great beauty. But beauty fades." She grinned, dropping her eyelids. She peered at herself from under two hoods. Her cobra look. She would never lose that. Thank God.

She heard the hoot of a tugboat, the roar of buses on the avenue and rummaging in her purse, she pulled out an empty cigarette pack. She entered a bar. She inserted coins into a vending machine and pulled the lever. A package dropped into her hand and she ripped off its top and thrust a cigarette between her lips. The bartender leaned over the counter, a book of matches in hand.

"They never put enough matches in those machines," he said. "Never." She lit her cigarette and sat at a small table. The bartender looked at her expectantly.

"Gin and tonic," she said, inhaling, leaning back, resting her head against the wall. A color TV hung over the bar with three men staring at its luminous surface. The bartender returned. "That will be ninety cents," he said, waiting as she opened her purse to hand him a dollar. He deposited a dime on the table and returned to the bar. An excited TV voice aroused the men, their enormous bodies swaying on the barstools, their shoulders pantomiming a fight as they jabbed and hooked, grunting with each blow. She felt wild, exultant feelings as the announcer described each blow until one boxer dropped to the canvas, the men screaming as the referee began counting and when she looked in the mirror behind the bar she saw the blood lust, the furies twisting mouths into mosaics of hate. Sudden waves of fear trembled her body as the referee counted and the men embraced, crashing fists down on the bar, celebrating this electronically transmitted violence that filled the room with a vicarious sense of triumph. The victor clasped his hands over his head, and, as she stared at the men, their behinds overlapping the bar stools, she suddenly felt sick.

Waves of nausea raised a sour acid taste that burned her throat and she rushed into the street to lean over the gutter, over the trash and excrement adding her contribution of bile, steadying herself against the pole, the overhead light casting a sodium vapor blur. Another convulsive spasm exploded in a choking burst until only a painful retching remained, her sobs now pumping a well gone dry.

Approaching headlights raced towards her as the horizon spun in a blur of blaring horns, screeching brakes, and voices shouting as she stepped out into the traffic, arms outstretched like a Goddess welcoming all who came to worship as she waved and nodded in majestic acknowledgement of each angry shout. She pounded her fist on the hoods of cars blocking her path as she staggered, head high, arms outstretched, across the street. She glared at angry faces, arms extended, single upthrust fingers proclaiming rage as she nodded in reply, unable to understand such protest. She struggled to maintain her precarious balance on the strangely tilted sidewalk.

She entered a liquor store and the man behind the counter did not smile. The storekeeper frowned as she navigated between shoals of bottles and baskets of wine to lean against the counter.

"I want a bottle of your best champagne," she

said, "Your very best." The merchant opened the cabinet and placed a bottle in a brown paper bag, stapling the top. He punched the cash register and handed her the change.

"Be careful on your way out," he said.

She stared at him, at his unmistakable look. "Fuck you!" she said, and then, honor restored, she paraded out the door, slamming it shut, the entrance bell jangling an echo of her anger.

The street was now steady, a corridor of lights and parked cars and ominous shadows concealing unknown dangers. She walked towards the corner listening to the sharp tapping of her heels, the casual rhythm of her footsteps somehow comforting, each musical phrase carrying her closer to the safety of brightly illuminated shop windows at the end of the block. She felt the chill of the champagne bottle, grasping the neck firmly, holding her purse against her side. Then she heard another sound, its rhythm alternating in ominous counterpoint to the tapping of her heels, quickening when she walked faster, slowing as she relaxed, hesitating when she paused to turn and stare at shadows that revealed nothing but the dark shapes of parked cars. She counted the streetlights to the corner, crossing the dark areas between them, listening to her footsteps, her senses sharpened by terrors concealed in the doorways and alleys between the buildings. Again she listened for and heard soft ominous sounds of footsteps alternating with her own. She stopped and looked back but again there was nothing to see, nothing but silence and shadows as she grasped the neck of the champagne bottle comforted by its solidity as if all her being now concentrated in her hand. She walked quickly to the next light, fighting panic, hearing footsteps running, remorseless fear converting dread into a steel spring of tightly wound fury waiting to explode, to lash out as she stopped abruptly and spun on her heels seeing a huge dark face lunging towards her, a sharp knife in an outstretched hand as she continued turning, arm extended, the neck of the bottle firm in her hand, its weight, its force increasing with each moment of acceleration as she screamed, driving all her strength and terror into this furious rotation, this frantic spin of her arms and shoulders arcing the bottle through the dark night multiplying its energy in one splintering blow against the side of a jaw, the bones breaking, the mouth opening in a twisted gasp of surprise, the knife flying from his hand, falling to the pavement as she again raised her arm bringing the bottle down against the side of a battered face, outstretched arms folding across his head, seeking protection as he sprawled helpless across the hood of a car, his eyes occluded with terror as she swung the bottle down as he rolled to one side, the glass pounding against steel, its fragments tearing the blood-smeared paper bag, a cold spray of champagne drenching her dress as she continued swinging through showers of champagne and glass as the bag burst and the unconscious man dropped to the gutter, his battered head wedged between two cars, blood streaming down his chest.

She stared at the broken jaw, at arms crossed in futile protection against undelivered blows as she released the broken bottle, the man choking on blood, the muscles of his legs spasming, his feet stirring as if some primal instinct urged him to rise from the pavement. She stepped back, withdrawing slowly, reluctantly, from the horror she had just consummated.

At the corner she raised her hand beckoning a cab swerving in to the curb. Opening the door she fell back into the seat, the wet dress clinging to her skin, the pungent odor of champagne filling the cab, the driver looking back quizzically. "Where to, ma'am?" he shouted through the grilled opening. He stared at her wet dress, the odor of alcohol undeniable.

"Lady," he said, "We ain't required by law to take drunks, ya know." He switched on the overhead light, illuminating the information placard on the back of his seat.

"Grand Central Station. Please!" she said as he shifted gears, cranking down his window, a cold draft flushing out the fumes as she shivered, hugging the wet dress to her breast.

EIGHT

She awoke on the couch emerging from a dreamless sleep, a trail of clothing marking her passage to the living room. She felt a cold hand on her naked breast and did not move, paralyzed with fear, the weight pressing down frustrating her desperate effort to scream, until gradually, she realized the hand was her own, her head pillowed on her arm cutting-off circulation. She stared at the ceiling, her terror dissipating, the streaks of light forming irregular patterns on the cracked plaster. She pulled a thin blanket around her neck, shivering, listening to the rumbling of a distant train amplified between walls of a rock cut carrying rails through the hills. Then she heard the sound change abruptly as the train entered a tunnel, piercing a huge bluff jutting out into the river, the sounds fading like a plaintive cry echoing her despair.

She looked out the window and saw trees rising from the frozen ground, bulky pyramids printed on the night sky, stark silhouettes against a horizon of hills, the lights on the far shore her only indication that she was not alone. She felt sweat under her arms, her fingernails digging into her flesh as she shut her eyes. The wool blanket was rough against naked flesh, and she imagined this is the way the world would end. Lonely horror. She began to tremble. The furnace hammered at corroded pipes distributing steam through the house, her heart counterpointing the heavy beat of trapped steam, small explosions bursting through air blocks, reverberations filling the house with creaks and groans and thumps that were like footsteps.

She opened her eyes watching condensation form on the windows, an opaque mist rising from radiators spreading hot air over cold glass, blurring her vision of sky and river and trees, dark shapes and silhouettes lurking beyond consciousness. Overhead she heard the shrill scream of a jet rising to a crescendo, acoustical agony scouring the countryside with reverberations that shattered her nerves on a schedule that was as regular as sunset and dawn. She listened as the roar overhead became a hushed rumble, then a solitary note hanging high in the sky with only the stars for audience.

She stood up hugging the blanket to her body and walked to the window looking down the pathway, a V-shaped notch in a cluster of stark and barren trees seeing stars through a maze of overlapping branches swaying in the wind, leaning over the water as if bent in prayer. She swayed with this movement as if connected somehow to the trees tracing branches across a skyline that merged with rolling hills and Palisades of rock. Then she saw indistinctly through mist-covered glass, a short, squat figure at the edge of the road staring up at the darkened house, entering the garden, walking down the inclined path, stopping to look up at the windows wandering among shrubbery and trees. Then the shadow stepped on to the cement walk, heels tapping as she clutched the blanket against her breast feeling her heart racing, the fear rising in her throat as she heard the doorknob turn, the door not opening with the outward pull of a strange hand. Then the figure disappeared, his footsteps fading behind the house and she heard the rear screen door swing open, the knob of the inside door tugging against the solid frame, and then, silence, only her breathing stirring atavistic fears with dark images of death.

She became a terrified animal with a hunter stalking just beyond a thin wooden door, and she imagined she could hear breathing, a hollow sound that paused before slithering away with an undulating motion that could have been wind rustling leaves banked-up against the house.

The furnace started, blotting out all other sound but the growl of vaporized oil burning in a hollow steel chamber in the basement as she walked to the couch, her eyes following that spectral image crossing the terrace, the hand reaching out to rattle a window in its frame as her heart raced and her knees weakened and she sat down huddling within the security of a wool blanket, a warmth that vanished as she heard another window rattling in its frame, metal screeching against metal driving fear into her heart. She listened to sounds circling the house, windows tested by a shadow reaching across opaque glass moving from door to window to door, a dark terror spiraling down deeper than it had ever traveled before into a wildly spinning maelstrom of horror, the room rotating into a void as she watched dark nothingness spread its diameter across the room and she rose from the couch, the blanket dropping to her feet, walking naked and erect to the closet, under the stairs, opening the door, reaching in to grasp the cold, gunmetal blue steel of an old target rifle, its wooden stock lightly oiled, the weapon balanced in her hand like an over-sized pistol as she turned towards the huge picture window framing the river, the mist-covered rectangle gray against a dark night sky that enclosed the house in a panorama of dread.

Now she saw through the window silhouettes of trees, one tall and thin, the other short and squat, two dark vertical blurs against opaque glass, the gap between them forming a notch looking down at the glassy smooth surface of the water that merged with the sky obliterating all sense of direction or depth with only a few stars disappearing as the opening between the trees suddenly filled with a moving figure approaching and pausing before trying to open the sliding door. She raised the rifle, arms trembling as she aimed the gun. She felt calm as she peered down the barrel centering the stub of the front sight in the deep V notch wavering before her eyes, squinting thru tears at the extended arm and shoulders and head of a dark blur tugging against the door. She could hear him swearing, his looming bulk at the window somehow penetrating her terror, stirring a familiar memory, a blurred image reaching her brain at the instant the slow, ever-increasing pressure of her finger squeezed the trigger, a shattering explosion of recognition arriving with the firing pin striking, the bullet spiraling, the cracking sound of a gun recoiling, a web of lines radiating across the window pane, a plug of glass flying outwards to the sky carrying with

these tiny crystalline shards her voice calling weakly,
"Steve?"

NINE

He saw a tongue of flame arcing from the gun instantly illuminating her face as jagged lines zig-zagged on the window glass, the rifle's high-pitched whine stabbing through his shoulder, ripping muscle, tendon and nerve, traveling across his body, shattering bone in a blazing fire of pain, his nerveless legs collapsing under him, his arms and head limp as the impact of the bullet spun him around, falling, hands outstretched, to the ground. He opened his mouth to call to her, a wordless, croaking sound spurting a red bubble between his lips, the salty, viscous taste of life flowing on to the frozen earth, a spreading pool of coagulating blood blackening as he felt himself drowning in encircling darkness.

He felt his cheek against a hard patch of soil that smelled of dirt and dung and he thought "My God! My God!" as he dug his fingers into the compost clutching a handful of earth as waves of pain spasmed across his back. "This is it!" he thought, I've had my ticket irrevocably punched for that final, everlasting journey, and isn't it stupid, really stupid when you think about it. The blackness and pain and the taste thickening in his throat intensified as he tried to speak but his words were garbled and never passed his lips, a voice deep within his spirit calling out as he tried to shout but the words faded, became indistinct and he was troubled because the message seemed important and he did not know what it was. If only I could concentrate, he told himself, but then his voice became a low moaning sound and he thought, "My God!" it's the wind coming off the river, moving through the trees, not a voice at all! No, that's the wind, definitely the wind, rubbing tree branches together, bare wood swaying with each gust. Yes, that's the wind, and then he saw in his mind, ripples traveling across the water moving slowly towards him, the wind forming small waves raising foamy whitecaps that flecked the water with spume, long streaks tracing the path of a warm wind blowing gently as if lifting and bearing him away, each puff slowly fading as he felt himself floating upon another river, the bubbling hiss of water trailing after his small, narrow craft as he reached out to the gunwales and pulled himself to the thwart, his head propped against the varnished wood as he looked downstream at the long, gradual bend just ahead, a white mist hanging over rocks jutting to the surface, the water tumbling over boulders, roaring through a narrow chute as he heard, in the distance, the heavy thunder of a waterfall.

The trees on the riverbank raced past, the water pounding the hull, the bow swinging downstream into the deeper and faster current following the outside arc of the river bend as he picked up a paddle grasping the hard, wooden shaft in his hands, his eyes searching for that tell-tale V-shaped pattern in the swiftly flowing current that indicated the safest passage through the broiling rapids. He held the blade above the water as the power of the current carried him downstream. With a powerful lunge he dipped into the white foam, turning the craft under the trees overhanging the river. The tumbling water bathed him in spray as he plunged through the cascading turbulence, the river widening, flowing fast and smooth, rounding the bend where he could see, above the trees, a cloud hovering over a waterfall tumbling down into the earth. He could hear water pounding on stone, the roar echoing through the forest, and he watched helpless as the river carried him towards a hazy line on the surface extending from shore to shore, the water disappearing into an enormous void where the river should be.

He thought how strange he no longer felt the pain across his back, his arm and shoulders swinging easily with each stroke, keeping time to the drumming of the falling stream that quickened as he pulled the blade through the water, the current flowing faster, the sound growing louder, the rhythm of the drumming rising to the frantic beat of a man possessed by this final journey over the brink where he could now see a cloud of mist changing shape above the void, transforming itself into a turbulent anvil-headed eruption of water turning white and then pink and then orange as it climbed skyward, reflecting the sun's lingering rays, an afterglow of golden warmth spreading across the horizon as he dug his paddle deeper into the stream. I know where I am going, he told himself, his heart pounding as the pull of his blade propelled him over the edge and into a cloud carrying him through a narrow canyon with steeply pitched walls opening and then moving together as he climbed over a short rise passing between mist-covered cliffs that leaned inward. He could see a wide valley, white rolling hills bordering a vast plain and he wondered where he had seen this terrain before, long parallel ridges shaped by prevailing winds raising small tufts of mist that flowed at right angles to his journey. Yes, it is somehow familiar and yet somehow changed, he thought as a tumbling avalanche came boiling down a slope and he watched the thick, sliding wedge carve a mountain in half, each separate hill moving apart forming a deep hollow in the endless plain.

Yes, I have been here before, he told himself, I know that slope, that hill, that mountain where the gullies form high above the timberline opening to the morning sun in huge snow-filled bowls just below that shoulder leading down from the summit. I know that mountain and oh what I wouldn't give to make that run just one more time. Just once more for luck, you know, for knowing the swiftest line down that peak it would be a sin to waste such knowledge. Yes, truly sinful, for that line can not be taught, each one of us must work it out alone and that is as it should be for there is no forgiving error or misjudgment that fails to lead you safely down from the summit crossing the enormous snowfield to the upper lip of the ravine where the pitch is almost vertical and as you lean into the slope your shoulder touches the snow racing past as you drop down and down and down faster and faster diagonally traversing the upper slope of the ravine that circles around you like a continuous wall of snow that drops endlessly down under you as you slowly rise, swinging up, out, around and down, your shoulders and arms moving powerfully in one long drifting turn, your skis carving a huge arc in the snow as you again sink into a low crouch, the wind burning your flesh as just ahead you see the stark trees of the timberline, frightening hazards surrounded by rocks guarding the approach to the Little Headwall that drops down into the forest in a sudden almost vertical pitch. Yes, there is no room for error, no misjudgment possible and, as you check your speed in one long sweeping turn through the floor of the ravine you are outside yourself in concentration and control, one brain and body fighting centrifugal force, your legs pressing down into the deep powder snow somehow solid as you lose speed, drifting and then edging your skis into a groove that drops you down right between the trees passing in a blur. Yes, you are the mountain and you are the wind racing down these slopes, and the trail through the timberline is the one path you follow if you can somehow keep your body and brain together, flesh and spirit inseparable following a vision unreeling in your head, for the sky and the snow and the trees possess you and you belong as much to them as to anything on this earth as snow blindness blots out everything but the images guiding you down the mountain.

It is a long, hard, climb up that trail, studying each corner, memorizing each checkpoint, imprinting on your brain the curves and straights you put together in your head memorizing that direct, unbroken line down the mountain as you swing up, out, around and down in a descent that concentrates all that you are, all that you will ever be for the moment when the sheer exultation of being alive is everything. Yes, there are moments when we are all one with everything and everything is in us and the mountains and the snow are the only reality and what we see and what we do, what we think and what we feel, are all one, solid, compact chunk of experience that somehow coheres moment by moment in the doing and the thinking and the feeling that is life itself. Yes, dear God, one more time down that mountain, one more run, one more thought, one final feeling and I will go gladly across those snowfields, up through those clouds where there is nothingness for your deadly work has already begun and in one-half of me there is now only memory. Only memory. Then for one brief moment he reached out and held his life in his hand, slowly turning it over again and again like a prism refracting light splitting the bright beam into many colors that merged into a dazzling white ray that pulsed with each beat of his heart telling him that he was not going to die for the light grew stronger and dying is always a fading away and he would never, no never, let go. Never.

Then he heard voices indistinctly as if in a dream, and as the voices became clearer he thought them somber, speaking in brief monosyllables that changed to hoarse whispers that he could not understand and when he opened his eyes he saw Helen standing next to his bed, her eyes neatly made-up, as they always were, thin, dark pencil lines underscoring the lids, a touch of shadow placed precisely, the entire effect emphasized by lines extending out of the corner of her eyes making them seem bigger and brighter and more alluring and he thought of her in front of the mirror working at her face with infinite patience, shading her eyebrows, blotting her lips in a perpetual ritual that each day achieved its purpose. He saw her smiling, and reaching out, he touched her hand, and then he remembered the crazy pattern of lines zig-zagging on the cracked window glass, felt the pain across his back, and tried to move.

"I want to wiggle my toes," he said.

A young doctor appeared. A smiling bright intelligence that spoke casually. "Just a pinched nerve, that's all. A nice, clean wound." The doctor held his wrist, looking at his watch. "A good strong pulse. Steady. You'll be just fine." Then, tucking the covers under Steve's arms, the Doctor picked up the pinchboard hanging at the foot of the bed and shuffled through the pages. "Fine. Just Fine." He nodded at Helen and went out the door trailing a strong odor of antiseptic handwash.

Steve noticed her nostril quiver as Helen turned from the door and pantomimed displeasure. "Smells like a drugstore, doesn't he?" Steve said.

"A hospital is not exactly a rose garden, is it?"

"I know."

"For a smelly doctor he does seem competent."

"Cheerful," he said. "Every morning they fill their white suits with cheer, just before making rounds." He was drowsy from medication and now a great hurt traveled across his shoulder as he tried to suppress a groan.

"Is it very bad?" she asked.

"I've had worse," he answered.

"Perhaps you should rest?" she said. "I don't want to tire you out."

"I just feel woozy," he said. "They're making me into a junkie."

"Very funny."

"What they gave me for pain must be good stuff," he said. "I feel great. Really do." He tried to raise his head from the pillow before falling back exhausted. His eyes closed and when they opened a smiling Helen was leaning over him.

"I'm glad you never learned to shoot straight," he said, as her face darkened, obliterating a smile. "I had no idea you were in the house."

"I was terrified. Thought you were a prowler."

"I know."

"If only you had called out. Or knocked."

"I forgot my key."

"I should have guessed it was you," she said, and for a moment she glanced down at his inert legs under the covers, her face softening into a look of misery. He watched her, thinking, this will never do, if it's going to be a long haul to recovery, compassion and pity and guilt will never do. They've got enough problems without that. He touched her hand.

"We're still friends."

"I was out of my mind with fear. Out of my mind."

"We haven't been smart. Only let's not go into that. And, maybe now things will change. What do you say?"

"I hope so."

"Bring me books and paper and pencils and I'm still in business. Doesn't matter where I write. OK?" He watched as she rummaged in her purse and withdrew a cigarette.

"Mind if I smoke?" she asked, striking a match, inhaling, her lower lip curling as she exhaled. She always dresses well he thought. Careful attention to what she wears. Yes, she looked great.

"You have the house all to yourself," he said.

"Do you mind?"

"No."

"You should invite someone to stay with you."

"I like being alone," she said. "I've lots of

thinking to do." She stabbed the air with the cigarette punctuating her words. "It will do me good."

"Hope so."

"I'll stay off the sauce if that's what you mean."

"That's what I mean," he said, turning away as the furtive little-girl look returned. He had spoken the unmentionable, broken the code that prohibited discussion of The Problem. Her hand fanned smoke from the cigarette and she seemed harried as she walked to the window and stared down at the street. At that moment she was vulnerable, trapped. He could guess what she felt whenever he mentioned drinking. Her shoulders sagged, self-assurance faded. Just thinking about drinking made her feel lost. No doubt about that. Yet not discussing The Problem was evasion. Denial. Make-believe. They lived a long-playing bad dream.

"I'm trying," she said. "Working at it. You know that better than anyone." She returned from the window and sat on the bed. "Talking makes things worse." Her eyes searched for an ashtray and then she reached to the bed table and jabbed out her cigarette.

"Maybe someday we can talk?" he said.

"I think not," she answered, lids dropping down over her eyes. Withdrawing. Her psychic dance. She would come on open and cheerful and direct and then he would reach out and touch the wrong nerve, stir the wrong feeling and that suspicious, frightened look would return and she would withdraw into herself where what he didn't know, what he didn't understand was killing their marriage. Yes, there was no doubt about it. He made her feel like a cornered animal by just talking. Yes, it was how he made her feel and she held him responsible for her feelings and of course she had these feelings long before they ever met. It was a closed circle she couldn't break out of except with a good stiff drink. One wrong word was all she needed to explode in drunken fury and rage. His words and her anger fed upon each other and so perhaps a pledge of silence did make sense after all. Withdrawing, pulling apart each day, was how they lived together.

"I keep hoping things will change," he said. She stared at him and he wondered if she understood what he was saying. "There's no future without change." She nodded. He lay back on the pillow and when he looked at her again she was crying. "I'm lucky to be alive," he said gently. "Too many accidents."

She leaned over and kissed him. "I have to go," she said. "See you tomorrow morning." He watched her button her coat, glancing into the wall mirror. She turned at the door and smiled. "Sorry about the tears," she said. "I know it's the last thing you want."

"Oh I wouldn't say that," he said. "A beautiful woman crying over me is not hard to take." He grinned.

She thought about this a moment. Then, without a word fled the room. He stared at the door, the feeling of something important somehow lost forever came over him as it always did whenever he attempted to speak to her. The truth is they no longer shared a common language and so the language they spoke was indifference and silence. Once she had been open, direct and totally honest and this had been her beauty, her rare, ravishing mark of distinction in a world where truth is clouded with a hazy tissue of lies and pretense. Now she had become furtive, covert, secretive and this was destroying her far more than alcohol for she was losing the very thing she once was as she traded-off an important piece of herself with each new deception. He loved her honesty but that was disappearing and when that was gone what was there to love but a memory of a beautiful dream?

He closed his eyes and slept, and when he awoke the doctor was standing next to him, a hypodermic held to the light, a dribble of fluid squirting from the needle as the doctor's arm arced down and he thought he felt a quick stab somewhere below his waist, the doctor studying his reaction asked "Did you feel anything?"

He withdrew the syringe, swabbing the puncture with a ball of cotton cooling the skin as the alcohol evaporated. "Did you feel anything at all?" the doctor said and he nodded, struggling through a drug-induced haze, his lips moving hesitantly.

"Cold," he said. "Cold."

The doctor grinned. "That's great," he said. "You'll be surprised how fast feeling will return. It's all a matter of time." Then writing on the chart, he turned and disappeared out the door, his footsteps fading down the hallway as darkness slowly filled the room.

TEN

The somber mood of the hospital traveled with her. The cold grey corridors crossed the threshold chilling the warmth of her home and she shivered as she removed her coat thinking a bath is what I need. Stumbling down the hall she scolded herself for not leaving a light on.

As she adjusted the taps her mood lightened, carefully testing water temperature she added bath oil while discarding clothes on the floor as steam moistened her face, streaking makeup as she sat on the edge of the tub. She poured half a glass of scotch, her spirits brightening as she postponed that moment when the first drink quieted the trembles that were as much a part of her as her name. She added water and lowered herself into the tub. Then, sipping slowly, she drained the glass, swinging her head from side to side as she worked kinks out of her neck.

She began to hum, trumpet sounds reverberating from the tile walls as she raised and lowered her glass in time to the beat. Then, she nodded, raising her glass in regal greeting to an unseen cheering throng, smiling as the final crescendo faded and she slid beneath the water, resting her head on the edge of the tub, closing her eyes to enjoy the weightless buoyancy floating her into a dreamy haze.

"Yes," she said, "I love you all. Daddy. Mommy. Steve. All of you. I love you all." Then the mist thickened as she groped for the bottle and refilled the glass. As she sipped her drink she could feel a tap tap tapping begin and this time it seemed to say Love, Love, Love, and in a moment she was on that beach, under a blazing sun, breathing the pungent odor of body oil and the sea, penetrating rays tanning her flesh transporting her into a semi-comatose state of ecstasy, her thirst increasing as heat dehydrated her enervated body sprawled on hot sand that held her lightly as any lover's embrace as she listened to the breakers sweeping on to the beach and then withdrawing with a prolonged hiss that sounded like a lover's sigh. Then she felt the morning breeze and as the air caressed her she shivered at its cooling touch pleasured by this sensation and it was then she recalled what Steve had said about off-shore breezes. She raised her head and looked at the edge of the sea watching her only child playing in a plastic boat, paddling with tiny hands, turning the small craft around and around and around, floating on to the sand with each wave and then receding into deeper water, shouting and waving at her as the sea ebbed and flooded on to the beach. She raised her hand in reply and then, squirting sun oil into her palm, she covered her arms and face spreading thick creamy lotion over her skin. She thought of Steve at the house behind the dunes pounding the typewriter, indoors on this, the most divine of all summer days, and then she remembered there was an out-going tide and for a moment she worried as the breeze freshened. Again she rolled over on her side and looked across the sand at the boat and child turning around and around paddling on and off the beach, floating on each new wave as the glassy surface of the sea advanced and receded. Far off-shore, sailboats drifted in the current, their limp sails somehow reassuring her all was calm as she yawned, watching her daughter paddling a small plastic boat at the edge of the sea.

Yes, all is calm, all is bright, only tomorrow is the fourth of July, not Christmas, and all she could look forward to was fireworks. Closing her eyes she saw rockets spiraling into the sky, exploding in bursting flowers of dazzling light, the roar of explosions booming out over the water as brightly illuminated patterns floated down towards the crowd and then she rolled on to her side, reaching for the oil, opening her eyes to look at the now deserted beach.

The wind and the outgoing tide created a chop with whitecaps parading out to sea, and as she ran to the water she spied the small plastic boat far off-shore. Frantic she watched as the wind and current carried the boat out towards the horizon and when the white hull disappeared behind the waves she turned and ran up the dunes towards the house, the sand sliding out from under her feet, gasping for breath, sharp pains knifing her lungs, and when at the crest of the dune she turned and looked out to sea, the boat was gone.

Every day for a week, Steve searched the surrounding waters, his face burning and then peeling and then burning again under a sun pitiless as the sea, his eyes staring from the bridge of a boat that followed the currents out into the open ocean before turning back towards the beach, never once sighting the child's body or that small, white plastic boat he had purchased at the local hardware store. After a week without food, without sleep, he became temporarily blind and abandoned the search. Yes, abandoned, Steve regaining his sight and returning to the keyboard which he would never, no never, abandon, not even on that fatal day on the beach when the sun was just about perfect and the wind so light you could hardly feel its touch until the sun, warming the land heated rising columns of air generating the goddamn lousy fucking off-shore breeze that just happened to coincide with that outgoing tide and that is what I mean by rotten stinkin' luck! Yes, she said, that was definitely bad luck. Helen's luck.

She groped for the bottle on the chair next to the tub and poured herself another drink. She listened to her heart beat, turning the animal around, hooves pawing the ground as his back arced, his shoulders and flanks trembling as her arm began swaying and swinging the cape. She made hollow sounds with her mouth, long drawn-out moans raising the animal's head as he trotted and then charged, lowering his horns as he came straight towards her now outstretched arm, his hooves pounding, his shoulders and flanks contracting, and then, reaching forward with each stride as she steadied the cape, bringing her arm in close to her hip, her voice rising in a drawn-out moan that rose higher and higher and higher as the bull lowered his head sweeping past in an upward hooking swinging movement of his horns that she met thrusting her groin out in one sudden voluptuous movement that jabbed the horn in deep, tearing flesh in an agonizing ecstasy that thrust her into the air, the horn withdrawing and then plunging in again and again and again, each new thrust enraging the animal, her moans rising higher and higher as the tearing cutting flame inside her spread beyond all consciousness of pain or pleasure. She looked down at her hand, and at the blood reddening the water, and she sobbed, shuddering spasms of anguish that ended after she dropped a broken glass on to the floor. "I'm hurt," she said, "I'm hurt," and she stared down at the pink water seeing a trickle of blood spread across the surface as she spasmed a painful hiccup that compelled her to hold her breath. She counted to ten, and then, gasping for air, she began to cry softly. "God damn Men," she said. "God damn fucking Men." Leave you bleeding and there's no one to clean up the mess. Never! Always trying to spurt that gummy sperm into you and there's no one to clean up the mess. No one. She sat up in the tub, raising her arms out of the water, carefully examining her wrists. She began to laugh. Not this time! Didn't do it this time and they will never do it to me again! Never. She ran her fingers down the insides of her arms, and then, she began to splash the bath water with her cupped hands, lifting it out of the tub on to the floor. "It's dirty dirty dirty," she said. "Very dirty. And no one wants it when it's dirty. Only when it's clean."

ELEVEN

"Well officer, I was sitting on this couch, sitting in the dark for I love to sit in the dark and let my thoughts run out where you can take a good look at what's bothering you, a necessary experience if you are not going to be driven out of your mind by what's going on deep down in that blessed unconscious that Doctor Fraud wrote all those books about. I suppose reading books is part of your training. Why I read in the Times that policemen are studying Spanish so they can relate with Hispanics. Of course I wasn't thinking that when I was on the couch, I was thinking kind of all-purpose thoughts you see because I had a horrible train ride that jangled my nerves.

As a matter of fact it is my habit when I get off that train to sit by the window to let the dust settle in my head for an hour. I sit quietly and listen to my pulse beating and all the sounds inside my head flow quietly. That's how I was, or about to be when you rang the doorbell. You see I have just returned from visiting my husband and I was upset because I had a terrible drive from the station with traffic coming at me from every direction. I thought maybe I would sit here and have a cigarette and a drink which I sometimes do as part of getting myself together when I am that way. I know you didn't mean to startle me when you rang the doorbell. I asked my husband to disconnect the wires, the telephone drives me straight up the wall and I suppose the way things are nowadays you must stay in touch and that means telephones and doorbells ringing when every nerve in your body is screaming riot and I don't blame you in the least for doing your job. You had no way of knowing what I have been through today. Hospitals are horrible and they say my husband's condition will improve rapidly as soon as the medications wear off.

Marvelous what they know. One look at a chart and it's all there on the computer. Marvelous. I was sitting here thinking about what they told me when I heard you at the door and I could not help thinking if he had only rung the doorbell but that is a might-have-been. You know of all the stories of Mice and Men the saddest is what might have been. Did they teach you that at the police academy? I like sayings. An investigator came the other day from the insurance company to tell me we have been having too many accidents, as a matter of fact they have already raised our insurance as far as it can go without actually classifying me accident-prone I think they call it. Accident prone! I guess I have been called just about everything. Some of my reviews would burn the paint right off the bar although there was a time when everybody had nothing but praise for my work. Superlative praise! But of course that was a long time ago. Before the world turned upside down with all those terrible assassinations. Right after they shot Kennedy I was so upset I forgot to set the handbrake and our car rolled down a hill. That's not accident prone! That's just being upset by all those killings. The Kennedys and then Martin Luther King and Malcolm X and all those boys in Vietnam it was like everybody who was beautiful was being killed off and anybody with a spark of decency just had to be troubled by what's happening. It got so bad I couldn't look at a newspaper or television without getting sick. Shit! It's not me that's accident-prone! Those smart-ass insurance guys should raise rates on the whole world! Do you know that? The world's a bad risk. Not me. All I did was sit on this couch. The lights were out because I like to sit in the dark. There's nothing accident prone about that, is there? Just sitting in the dark, Officer. Just thinking deep thoughts. You know the kind when you are so far inside yourself you don't care if you ever come back for another look at all the misery that's everywhere. You know what I am talking about. I read a book about cops. Or is it firemen? The horrors you guys see, day after day, year after year. I don't know how you manage to keep sane. It's not easy is it? That's why my nerves start screaming. When I heard that sound at my door it was like a bomb going-off! The whole house was quiet. Everything was creaking and groaning and then suddenly at the back door someone was trying to break in. Sounded that loud. Goddamn footsteps. Like a Frankenstein movie.

I heard him circle the house. Then he tries climbing through a window. How the hell was I to know he had forgotten his key? Wasn't feeling well. Had such a terrible time in the city. The train ride. The drive. Then, just as I am about to get myself together he tries ripping the back door off its hinges and goes clomping around the garden to the rear window. I didn't mean to hit him. Just wanted to scare him away. Couldn't hit the side of a barn with a beach ball. Pulled the trigger and there was my husband on the terrace and here I am trying to explain to insurance investigators and policemen what is really quite apparent if only they would look at the situation. Guess that's how it is. First they call me accident-prone and no telling what they're going to say now. Well let me tell you what I really am. What I really am is fed-up. Fed-up right to here with all this crap. If you really think I tried to murder my husband why the hell don't you come right out and say so? I pulled the trigger. Shit! He's loaded with insurance. A great motive. So why the hell don't you lock me up instead of barging in on me after I've had such a rough day? I mean how much do you think I can take? I don't like questions. Questions are an impertinence. There's no way of asking questions without being rude. You're impertinent and what's more you know it was an accident even though I am not accident-prone whatever the insurance investigator says. I am just me. Little-Old-Me living in an accident-prone world and if my husband had not forgotten his key or had the sense to ring the doorbell I would not be talking to you today. No way. God, the people I find myself talking to when I'm drained. Hardly enough energy to drive to the hospital with everybody demanding my time and everything that makes living in this Godforsaken world possible. I'm very tired. Sometimes so tired I don't think I can speak or move or even breathe another breath and here I am answering all your questions. I am cooperative, am I not? You seem like you know what I'm saying, as if you understand people who have lived their lives inside a nightmare that suddenly becomes real and looks up at you from a hospital bed. That's certainly real, isn't it? Isn't it real when someone is almost killed? God, there are so few real things happening today I guess a little accidental manslaughter is needed every now and then to remind us we are alive. What do you think? You certainly don't do much talking, do you? I thought detectives are supposed to ask questions? Christ you haven't opened your mouth since you sat down. What I am trying to say is I am sorry it happened. It was stupid of me. And what is worse I can't understand why I was so quick to pull the trigger. I was shooting at a shadow. The story of my life. Everything I have been terrified of turned out to be shadows. Do you think that's why I drink? Your opinion is as good as anyone else's. Believe me I've been to the best Shrinks and they just don't know what it is like to be me. To be locked up with shadows dancing on the walls. Like that song about dancing on the ceiling that keeps going around and around inside my head. Do you know that song? It's the story of my life. Shadows dancing on the ceiling. Only I am that shadow swaying back and forth, turning around and around, keeping time to as lovely a tune as ever I have heard. My favorite song. Acting was a mistake. What I am is a born dancer. Shit. My mother dragged me in and out of agent's offices before I was ten. Dancing. That's what I am, really. Dancing, that's me. Not that stage crap playing phony parts in cardboard plays by hacks like my husband. No wonder I started drinking. Believe me there's more artistry, more feeling, more dramatic power in one simple turn across the stage then in all the empty-headed parts I played in vulgar service to my so-called success. I was almost a star did you know that? My acting coach said I had greatness only they didn't tell me there were damn few great parts for my greatness to play. My mother believed every goddamn thing they said. And there was no money in dancing. Even if you were Isadora Duncan! She died dead broke and dead drunk and I suppose she was my idol when I was young playing lousy little walk-on parts for fifty bucks a week. God there's no undoing the mess we make of our lives. Only I didn't make this mess. Other people made it for me. All I did was play the part they gave me in a flop! Shouldn't run two nights. Yet it goes on forever! Forever! My problem is I don't know how to bring the curtain down. Not that I didn't consider it every now and then like the time I lost my child. Drowned. In the ocean. But that's another story. That husband of mine is never there when you need him. Never. Just half a man living half a life in that goddamn mind of his chewing away at what ever he's got in his head. Christ! If only I knew then what I know now after living a half life for more than half my life. Marriage is worse than anyone admits. Marriage has ruined more lives than cancer! At least they can cut the damn thing out without tearing you into little bits. People do tear, you know. They tear into bloody little pieces if they lack the guts to split. Either way you just can't win. Fat or thin you just can't win. Married or single too, I guess. None of us are programmed for success. It's just not natural. It's a lie we tell ourselves, like children lost in the dark, filled with dread. Our hair turns grey and our feelings bitter and that my friend is what life is all about. Once you've learned that secret all that's left to discuss is sex. Screwing. Fucking. Copulating. Rutting.

Making love. Making push-push. Making bang bang! Humping! Fornicating! You know, the good old group-grunt! Mass ass! Gang bang! Circle Jerk! And now, that most sophisticated indoor sport, swinging! As dread closes in we dive head-first into a bottle or make a career of mental illness. I prefer a well-made martini! You can only spend so much of your life trying to make contact and when the world stops smiling back, when these four walls do not contain someone you love, well that's a disaster I wouldn't wish on a dog! I mean a dog has more feeling, more loyalty, more devotion. I've never heard of dogs doing what we inflict on those we love. Have you? Huh? Say something! Don't sit there like God! I mean you asked me questions and I am trying to answer and you know it's not easy. You know that, don't you? I mean how the hell should I know why I pulled the trigger? I knew it was my husband the moment I shot him. I called out his name just as the gun fired, so help me God it was still an accident even though as I walked out on the terrace I was hoping it was him. I wasn't quite sure but you know the way he reached for the window was familiar. You live with a man long enough and you even know how he breathes. Hell I put myself to sleep counting the rhythms of his breathing. Sleeping with a man for what seems a lifetime you become strangers, people who don't really know each other and so you just lay there watching the blanket rise and fall. Jesus Christ when he reaches out to touch me it's absolutely obscene in the truest, fullest, most accurate meaning of that word. Obscene! If you are any kind of a person, you know, if you are not hanging back with the apes there is only just so much obscenity you can stand without being driven up the wall. I wanted to murder him many times. But that doesn't make me a murderess does it? A stranger touches you in the street. Reaches out and fondles your breast or pinches your ass like they do in Italy. You slap his face and that's that. But when it happens in bed with your husband you just can't lay there and take it! Sooner or later you strike back. Throw dishes. Slam doors. Every thing you do is one more triumph in your arsenal of vindictiveness. Murder is too painless. Believe me the only thing that truly satisfies is torment. Wives only murder their husbands by accident. The alternatives are so much more satisfying."

TWELVE

Steve Irwin rolled the chair from his desk and looked across the room at the far wall of his study. He glanced at the books on the shelves. Yes, third from the end, on the top shelf was the one he wanted. In one month he had won the right to scrupulously maintain self-reliance. His working rhythms had returned. Each morning he closed his door secure in the promise of no intrusions. The nervous disquiet of the hospital had been distilled into the rigorous discipline of work. Gone was inactivity, fattening body and soul, clogging brain and spiritual plumbing. Now he would cross the room and get that book.

An achievement a day.

Grasping the arm of the wheelchair he lowered himself to the floor dragging his legs, heels tracing parallel tracks on the rug. After resting a moment, he pressed down again, raising his body, legs trailing after him as he propelled himself across the room, hands pushing against the floor as he swung up, back and down pivoting from his shoulders in the rocking motion of an infant crawling to his destination. He looked past the desk at the wheelchair and typewriter.

Silent as the Sphinx.

At the wall he had constructed steps rising to the middle shelves. There a narrow platform and a long pole made his books accessible. With a down-thrusting of both hands, he climbed up the stairs, raising himself, arms trembling, step by step, concentrating his strength in a steady sequence of pressing and raising and sliding as he struggled to the platform.

Mount Everest.

He alone sawed the two by fours, trimmed the white pine plank steps, hammered nails through wooden beams into the oak floor. He measured and cut diagonals for bracing, wedging and nailing them into position, slowly building a plywood platform. He also constructed inclined ramps to the garden and garage. Working alone, he rejected all offers of assistance.

Squeezing the lever controlling two metal fingers at the end of a long pole, he slid a book to the edge of the shelf. Grasping it firmly, he lowered the book to his lap. Then he descended the stairs, hands cushioning the wooden steps.

Placing the book on the desk, he raised himself from the floor into the wheelchair. He reached down and lifted his legs on to the footrests before turning to the typewriter.

Mission accomplished.

His writing rhythms returned. The feelings spasming out of him in bursts of savage joy filled his days. The surge of words renewed, acquiring a momentum, a vitality all their own. Some days he hated his work. On others, the fog lifted from his mind and he was grateful for each page. But neither gratitude nor hate made a difference. He was, he knew, in perpetual bondage to the words and feelings flowing from his fingertips. Some days he felt close, and on others, quite distant from his writing which was inseparable from his life. His work was an old friend forever presenting him with revelations and mysteries that were an endless source of delight and wonder. If his world did have a circumference, if his life did contain meaning, he would someday touch that circumference, distill that meaning by writing harder and longer and more fiercely than he had ever written before. His mind, was difficult to contain, but under the net of his daily discipline it would lead him to the center of his life. That center around which his existence revolved. There was within him a focus, a deep guiding principal that governed all. He struggled to reach that center to discover the circumference of the circle that contained his world. And with this hard-won knowledge he could, perhaps, survive.

He often felt he lived in a cave deep within himself, and in that recess there were memories of a past that engaged the present in perpetual interrogation. A questioning boy continually asking, "Why?" the man talking to himself when young, enfolding and shaping his life by listening and remembering. That is all. Just listening and remembering and writing.

He opened the book, an illustrated textbook and turned to the chapter on paralysis to read about recovery of function. Yet, he had not recovered. Why? He studied the nerve bundles descending the legs, branching from the base of the spine. His nerves were alive. Healthy. Undamaged. Yet their trauma had been so intense they no longer transmitted commands from his brain. Why? Why the block? He concentrated on vague feelings in his atrophying muscles. Yes, there is no specific therapy other than massage and passive exercise to prevent contractures. What the hell are contractures? He opened a medical dictionary. Contractures are a shortening of a muscle or tendon so that it can not be straightened or flexed and extended. Jesus Christ! What if when nerve transmissions were restored there were no muscles left to function? The mind was a crippler. Always playing dirty little games.

He spun the wheels on the chair and rolled down an inclined ramp into the garden. There he laced-on leg braces attaching them at knees and ankles with wide leather straps. Straightening his legs, he locked the knee joints.

Pushing down on the arms of the wheelchair he rose to his feet. Taking the pair of crutches leaning against the wall, he slid them under his arms. Time to walk. A mile a day.

Grasping the crutches he moved ahead, raising and swinging his legs under him. Again and again he leaned forward and swung his legs forward with the thrust of his shoulders bearing down on the crutches. Balancing on his two feet he raised the tips. His steel-braced, unfeeling legs swung from his hips as he crossed the garden to the road and back, again and again until the day his nerve-endings resumed transmitting.

If his nerves refused to send orders to his legs could he not reverse this block by repetitive activity of flaccid muscles, reopening pathways to his brain? Severe shock had scrambled the memory bank that enabled his brain to transmit that complex pattern of chemical and electrical messages called walking. Could he restore this activity? Revive this chemical and electrical pattern? Speech is relearned by the muscles of the tongue, one sound, one syllable at a time. Months of training are required to relearn words after a stroke or other brain damage. Is not walking less complex than speech? A simple muscular activity with no thoughts or images or feelings involved?

He moved ahead, swinging his legs up forward and down again and again. He maintained a steady rhythm, his arms and shoulders shifting his weight. Halfway to the road, he rested. Then he concentrated on his right side focusing attention on his thigh and calf. He raised one crutch, lifting its rubber tip off the ground, and waited. The immobilized leg was dead weight attached to his hip. Inert flesh encased in leather and steel. He closed his eyes and visualized bundles of nerves shown in brightly colored illustrations in the medical textbook.

Not a flicker.

He lowered the crutches and concentrated on his other leg. He believed he felt warmth in his thigh. He focused his mind on that muscle, jaws clenched, teeth grating.

Again he balanced himself between crutches and walked towards the road, raising and swinging his legs under him, reaching forward each time his feet touched the ground. He would stand erect for a moment and then, tottering, almost falling, swing the crutches ahead in long strides with his powerful arms and shoulders thrusting down and back, step by step.

Move goddamnit! Move!

He concentrated on his back and stomach muscles. Lifeless below the waist. Arriving at the road he rested, his breathing labored, his face wet with tears of frustration. He balanced on rigid legs and then, holding the crutches away from his body, he released his grip and the crutches fell to the ground.

Again he concentrated on the bundle of nerves down his spine, branching out to his legs. He traced one sensation following an imaginary transmission to his lower body. He could travel just so far with his mind. He reached down with both hands and moved his right leg forward. Then, standing erect to regain balance, he rested. Then he reached down and repeated the same movement with his left. Right. Left. Rest. Right. Left. Rest. Right. Left. Rest.

Three feet.

Six feet.

Nine feet.

He was now at the road. How the hell do you turn around? He paused at the edge of the blacktop. Not bad. How far had he gone? A hundred yards? A hundred fifty? Not to be confused with walking. Still it was a hell of a lot better than sitting on your ass. OK? Turn-around time.

He reached down and moved his right leg back, half a step. Then, without hesitating, he reached down and moved his left leg forward half a step. He repeated these movements until, facing the house, he tottered, struggling for balance, standing erect, sweat darkening his shirt.

Hundred fifty yards. Shit! More like two hundred! That's four, maybe five hundred steps to the house. The sun directly in his eyes. He began to tremble. A breeze cooled his wet back. He must concentrate. Keep focused. He would make it if he kept working at it, step by step. One movement at a time. Like flying. Follow the checklist. The balance of your body is in your head. Look at the ground and you'll fall on your face. Look at the sky and you'll fall on your ass.

He alternately moved each leg forward, reaching down to set the braces in position. Prehistoric creatures crawling from the primordial ooze first stood erect and learned to walk this way. Sea creatures reconsidering this evolutionary step returned to the sea where they weightlessly wagged their tails. But what choice did he have? Walk? Or roll around in a chromium-plated chair? He must try swimming. FDR was a swimmer. Warm Springs and the White House. Great for the arms and shoulders. Left. Right. Rest. Left. Right. Rest. Yes, swimming was the way to go.

He stopped at the crutches lying on the ground and considered using them.

"May I help, Mr. Irwin?"

He looked over his shoulder at a young woman carrying a valise. Medium height. Tan raincoat. Yes, he recognized her. The hospital. The nurse. The one with the French name.

"Miss Bousquet?"

"Yes, Mr. Irwin." She lifted the crutches off the ground sliding them under his arm.

"You were quite a sight."

"You should see me dance."

"Not today. Not for a while, please."

He swung forward towards the house and then turned with a grin. "What we asked for was that big Swede physio-therapist to work hell out of my legs."

"The hospital sent me, Mr. Irwin. Whirlpools, weight-lifting and massage. The big Swede's now on TV. A professional wrestler."

He shuffled forward, moving in rhythmic swings. Leaning the crutches against the wall, he bent down and unlocked the knee joints before sitting in the wheelchair.

"I have only one rule," he said. "Never touch this chair, unlock my braces, or hand me those damn crutches or anything else I need. Ever! Stay the hell out of my way when I am working, and when I drop something nobody but me picks it up. Understand?"

"Yes Mr. Irwin."

"Why the hell did you take this rotten job?'

"It's better than bedpans, meal trays and taking temperatures every hour. There's a shortage of orthopedic nurses. I need the experience. I hope to work in the children's ward someday."

"Well," he grinned. "You've come to the right place."

"I've been warned."

He stared at her a moment. "Good seeing you," he said.

THIRTEEN

When innocence is lost and a soul runs dry our world changes. Orthopedic nurse Anne Bousquet, abandoning the Maryknoll Order, pondered a future she could hardly imagine. A future of choices free of the church's discipline and security. Now, after twenty years of dedicated service she determined to live an unconsecrated life. Free and indivisible.

"Our father who art in heaven, I want to live," she prayed. "Hallowed be thy name, a life worth living and I don't mean merely exist. Thy will be done. Thy kingdom come, I want to live. Yes, on earth as it is in heaven. Yes, I want to live before I die. Amen."

Anne Bousquet's heart chilled returning to Maryknoll to renounce her vocation. Despair compelled her to abandon all she had vowed prostrated on the seminary's cold stone floor. A bereft Sister Anne now asked what have I done with my life? What will fill the emptiness I feel? Fleeing from unbearable horror I turned coward. Unable to tolerate atrocities, I lost courage. For without absolute faith, courage dissolves, never to return.

Only a muffled bell's mournful tolling replied. The

granite seminary building glowed in the morning's golden light as the rising sun painted the Palisades on the river's far shore. A train's clatter raced through the valley intensifying her disquiet. A jet rumbled overhead tracing contrails across the sky like the moving finger of God. She closed her eyes and listened to the wind rustling treetops. The beloved wind that once had transfigured her life.

As a young girl she climbed an apple tree in her father's orchard, and on a high branch surveyed a wilderness populated by imaginary beasts and Indians and unseen dangers. Lake Champlain extended miles north of her perch. Wooded shores with no farmhouse in view. She felt exultation watching shadows turn daylight to dusk as a gentle wind formed ripples on Champlain's mirrored surface. Ripples became waves as a breeze creased the water forming whitecaps. Birch trees on the distant shore bent over to touch the ground like supplicants at prayer as she trembled before the unseen power swaying fields of goldenrod and wheat. A soft breath of air touched her face, a caress ruffled her hair as an invisible hand brushed away fear. Trembling ceased. She felt ecstasy.

For several hours she waited for wind to ripple the water anticipating waves that never formed as overhead cumulus clouds expanded into exotic shapes. Whitecaps appeared and when nearby, a grove of birch trees trembled, she shivered. Her vigil continued until evening shadows darkened the surface of the lake as a line of majestic thunderheads marched across the sky.

A violent storm. Trees uprooted, over-ripe fruit fell to the ground, lightning flashed. Blinded by tears she cried out at this wonder and never again did she feel wind on her cheek, gaze at the sky or look out over the water unmoved.

Yes, Sister Anne admitted, the wind no longer responds to my prayers yet that young girl still lives enthralled by clouds sailing across the heavens; still waits, trembling, for the gentle touch of the hand of God.

Yet, it was the hand of man and not God that threatened the Santa Magdalena Mission, built in the Columbian highlands by Soldiers of Christ, lured two hundred miles inland by piety and greed. Centuries later, settlers invaded the valley to slash and burn the rain forest and kill Indians for sport. Their savagery shattered Sister Anne. Her hope for the Mission's survival faded when an ancient paddlewheel riverboat debarked soldiers at the village. The terrified Indians fled. Sister Anne gathered up her skirts and followed them into the jungle.

Threatening shadows obscured the trail. The haunting cry of macaws in the rain forest's canopy counter pointed the chatter of machine guns. Choking on cordite fumes, stumbling through a tangled mangrove forest, Sister Anne ran towards the sound of exploding grenades shouting "You must not kill! You must not kill!" to soldiers ordered to kill and keep on killing. Drained by the humid jungle heat, she staggered on, devastated, collapsing into prolonged darkness.

Awakening, she recalled the burned-out marketplace, women and children pleading for mercy, soldiers reloading, firing and reloading again and again. Charred debris from burning huts drifted down from the sky covering the dead under a gray ash shroud. Searching the village for survivors, Sister Anne stopped to shield a child in her arms, her cries unheard amidst the gunfire. Shards of bloody flesh splattered her cassock as a rampaging soldier bayoneted the mother cowering beside her. Sister Anne raised her fist and cursed God.

Awakening, she listened to surf pounding the beach outside her hospital room, wondering how long she had been asleep. She was surprised to learn her time of darkness lasted three months.

Father Carlos opened the window curtain flooding Sister Anne's room with sunlight. He sat beside her, his enormous bulk overflowing a small chair. He raised a hand. Two thick jowls bulged over his starched white collar as he blessed her.

"You'll soon be well, Sister Anne. With God's mercy you'll return to the mission stronger than ever."

Sister Anne raised her head from the pillow. Her eyes slowly adjusting to the light. She recognized her visitor and whispered, "No father, I will never return to Santa Magdalena."

The old priest hesitated. His voice comforting. "I will pray you forget the unspeakable horror you survived."

Sister Anne closed her eyes. "Never," she said. Her voice fading. "Never."

Father Carlos flushed. His face crimson. "What good can come remembering? Dwell on evil and you live with it forever."

Sister Anne remained silent. Then, her voice weak, eyes clearing of sleep she said, "Some wounds never heal, father. Remembering has a purpose."

"And what is that, Sister?"

"Redemption."

Surprised, the Priest suppressed a tolerant smile.

"Redemption?" he asked. "Redemption?"

"Yes, father. So the dead will not perish again when we forget them."

Father Carlos rose from the chair. Walked to the window. Turning from Sister Anne, he gazed out at the sea. Hesitating. Thoughtful. His voice firm, he said "Grievous wounds must drain before healing is possible."

Her voice insistent, Sister Anne replied, "With respect, father, I don't agree."

Startled, Father Carlos turned from the window, his voice asserting authority. "My child, you have no choice. You took holy vows."

Sister Anne's head fell back on the pillow. She stared at Father Carlos, pausing before speaking. "A promise I can not keep," she said softly. "I have no choice."

Father Carlos leaned closer to the bed as if he had not heard her. "Are you certain that is in your heart?"

"Yes Father."

Father Carlos lowered his voice. His sad eyes fixed on Sister Anne. "But that is not possible," he said. "A vocation can not be spit out like a piece of bitter fruit. Devotion, discipline, sacrifice will not always taste sweet. With time, faith returns to one who believes in God's mercy. Wait until you are well, Sister Anne, before you make such an important decision. Remember, what is good always revives."

"And what if what revives is not good?"

"Judge not what is beyond our understanding."

Sister Anne raised a hand. Her voice insistent. "But I do understand, father. I understand quite well. I have had my answer. I no longer can serve God."

"What are you saying, my child?"

"I am no shaman, father. No holy man exploiting ignorance to save souls."

The Old Priest frowned. Searching for a reply. He nodded. "True. Your healing power comes from penicillin. A miracle to those ignorant of science. And yes, the Indians bless you for saving their lives and yes, you failed them when the soldiers came, failed them as I have failed you."

"I have failed no one but myself."

Father Carlos stepped from the window. Reaching out to hold her hand. Concern clouding his voice. Pleading.

"Do not blame yourself because the natives worship you. Do not reject their belief in you. Do not renounce what you alone can give them."

"I want to be free of that burden. I no longer can bear it."

"You will never be free. Never! You have been called to do God's work and can not refuse."

Sister Anne held back tears. "I can no longer live with their belief in me, Father. I am unworthy of their faith. I am a fraud."

FOURTEEN

Yes! Not just the penicillin, but the healing power of touch. The laying on of hands. God's great gift. Hands that seemed more magical than the wine and host of the eucharist.

A power to be used with humility.

To the Indians, convinced Sister Anne was a shaman descended from the sky to take temperatures, give injections and probe their emaciated bodies, each surviving infant or healed wound confirmed her divinity. Silently watching her treat their suppurating sores, the Indians were grateful believers. Sister Anne shared their intense joy in the miracle of touch when recalling her cloistered life shunning all physical contact. To be deprived of this mute language, where neither a handshake nor an embrace were permitted, was a deprivation greater than keeping perpetual silence. Arriving at Santa Magdalena armed only with avid faith and a suitcase of antibiotics, Sister Anne felt herself guided by overwhelming love. Pleased by the child-like Indians' gratitude, she enjoyed their adoration. A sin of pride she dared not confess to Father Carlos. As were other troubled thoughts.

Witnessing nights of orgiastic feasting, abandoned dancing and shameless public copulations aroused disturbing feelings. She recognized that naked lust was followed by tenderness to infants, wives, and the aged. A love vital as the love of God. Yet without love of each other, the love of God seemed barren. Unsatisfying. And, if this was true, then the vows she must keep were vows of incompleteness. Being less than fully human.

To escape the disturbing sight of orgies, Sister Anne fled to the river to watch traffic flowing downstream on the mud brown water. Emerging out of the mist on uprooted trees and other flotsam, wild jungle animals, surviving the seasonal flood reminded her of dangers that seemed unreal. What was real, however, was her dwindling supply of antibiotics, vaccines, aspirin and bandages. What could not be ignored and must be served were mothers crowding the clinic as she examined infant's eyes, ears, and throats for trachoma, yaws, and blackwater fever. And yes, far beyond the magic touch of her hands were the terminally ill ravaged by parasites and unknown infections.

If she were truly a God the Indians believed in - what miracles could she perform? Yes. A most sinful thought requiring many Hail Marys and Mea Culpas for forgiveness. Watching bedridden Indians turn their faces to the wall of their huts and die without a word of reproach or complaint, she prayed for more penicillin and its God-like power.

FIFTEEN

Bless, baptize and bury. Bless, baptize and bury. The dedicated duties of a missionary priest also included enduring torrential rain, mudslides and drought. Performing holy sacraments offered little consolation to Father Carlos struggling to teach Indians to terrace hillsides to hold topsoil. Disappointing harvests produced little more than famine's pitiless signature. Spindly legs and swollen malnutrition bellies. Resigned to failure, Father Carlos gracefully wore the humility of defeat.

Denounced as a "comunista", a threat to church and state, though an inspiration to university students, Father Carlos was assigned to Santa Magdalena to preach his "Liberation" heresies to the rain forest. A silenced Father Carlos now did penance for his convictions and the damage they may have done. For as the bishop of Bogata proclaimed when exiling him to the jungle - God alone is the final judge of good or evil and Father Carlos was but a misguided missionary priest.

Father Carlos did not reply. Did not say to his confessor, "There is no need to forgive me for I have

135

not sinned. Have not blasphemed. Have not preached heresies to the hungry, the ill, the poor who will always be with us as long as the church serves best those who need it least. A church that denies the tortures, murders, disappearances, and exterminations committed in its name has lost its way. Become morally blinded by power and wealth. And, like my church, I have grown old and fat. However, my failing eyes see more than ever before. See that living a loving and caring life is beyond church rituals. Beyond its authority. And what I must confess is a lost faith in an institution I no longer approve of. A church that will never change."

Father Carlos's was encouraged by the arrival of Brother Maurice, Santa Magdalena's carpenter and electrician. An eager French Canadian with a canvas tool bag at his waist and a sparse beard darkening a boyish face. With the belfry stairs a hazard, and the ancient generator inoperative, Brother Maurice would be a welcome addition to the mission. Undaunted by hard work or the jungle's dangers, Brother Maurice set new tiles on the roof, repaired the belfry stairs, and cleaned the generator's fuel injectors restoring light to Santa Magdalena. A most cheerful sight to behold. Father Carlos admired the young man's empathy listening to the Indians chanting their stories, applauding as they boasted of raids on other villages during the "Violencia" years. Stamping his feet as he danced and shouted with the natives, Brother Maurice seemed a great good gift. Exactly what the mission needed to do God's work.

Brother Maurice's presence also coincided with the appearance of a perplexing mystery. The heartbreaking sight of grapes rotting on the ground in Father Carlos' beloved arbor. The strings supporting the precious vines were stolen by Indians, who habitually sharing their possessions, had no concept of personal property. Seeing natives wearing string necklaces and colorful bracelets Father Carlos thought them possessed by an unholy passion. For the string seemed a sacred talisman. A grievous sin to be ruthlessly purged.

One evening, walking the footpath beside the river Father Carlos encountered Indians crowding around Brother Maurice. They chattered expectantly as Brother Maurice held up a short length of string, the ends joined with a knot forming a small loop. Brother Maurice handed the looped string to the natives asking them to test the knot. Raising the string aloft, Brother Maurice cut the side opposite the knot, severing the loop. He then wrapped the string around the palm of his hand, concealing the knot in his fist. Brother Maurice held out his hand, displaying the string wrapped around his palm, a short length dangling from his closed fist.

Fascinated, the silent Indians crowded closer staring at his hand. Brother Maurice asked one to come forward and grasp the length of string dangling beneath his fist. A young man stepped from the crowd, reached out and pulled the end of the string unwrapping it from Brother Maurice's open hand.

Astonished, The Indians stamped their feet, shouting approval. Brother Maurice held up both hands. The knot concealed in his fist had vanished. Awestruck. Silent. The young Indian held aloft his prize. The now magically uncut string. A sacred talisman.

Father Carlos concluded there was more to Brother Maurice than magic tricks and yes, his high spirits and songs would be missed if he was banished. Innocence was his true vocation. Purity of soul that opened hearts. How cruel to discipline him for being as child-like as the Indians.

Brother Maurice appeared unhurried, composed, proud, his walk proclaiming, "For better or worse I am a man." And, after twenty years at Santa Magdalena Sister Anne felt the need to talk to someone new. Someone whose arrival evoked an awakening. And yes, she thought, along with songs and conjurors tricks, Brother Maurice was truly a man from that almost forgotten world outside the mission walls. For Sister Anne knew how to be alone, but not how to be delivered from the anguish of loneliness. She yearned to find someone from whom she would never stop receiving, and to whom she would never stop sharing her soul's sacred mysteries.

Father Carlos was not that man. An old priest, straining with failing eyesight to read his breviary, with whom she did not recall one personal conversation, one flow of words to dispel the loneliness wasting her heart.

To her delight Brother Maurice was an avid story-teller. The hours traveling upriver to visit outlying villages passed quickly as he told of his childhood, of cruel arctic winds killing children walking to school, of savage winters, and poverty and starvation and epidemics that decimated entire families; the young abandoning parents and grandparents, with only a church to comfort their lonely years. He told of hunting and fishing on Quebec's rivers and lakes. Wild freedom despite poverty. Of a starvation winter and being rescued by an Inuit tribe; a hunting trip aborted by an early freeze-up. He spoke of hearing the shamans' stories reaching back to Time's beginning telling of ancestors hunting the seal and the caribou, and never knowing hunger. The shamans sang of the first woman given to man to cook and sew and birth sons who became great hunters, and how each year caribou herds appeared as far as the eye could see. Food was plentiful until the time no caribou herds came, and death claimed all but a few who never understood their fate. Why did so many Inuit die? Why did the owl, the sacred messenger of the underworld call out so many names?

Drifting with the current in the fading twilight Sister Anne and Brother Maurice watched the setting sun paint the mission a soft pink, then lavender, then a glimmer of red before the walls vanished from sight in the gathering dusk. The stars overhead glowed gently. Mute before the wonder of tropical beauty they were voyagers crossing a sea of mystery to an unknown destination where other images surfaced.

Brother Maurice's somber face darkened as the canoe floated with the current like a reed in the wind. Only the sound of lapping water, bird songs and monkey chatter intruded upon the silence.

Brother Maurice steadied the canoe in the swift current. Sister Anne turned and staring at him asked, "Yes, Why?"

Brother Maurice remained silent paddling towards shore. "You know the answer," he said. "The oldest story ever told."

"I can guess," Sister Anne said smiling at what came to mind.

"A woman, fig-leafed Eve. Blamed for Adam's troubles."

Brother Maurice laughing, recited, "Fig-leafed

wench, hussy crone, thou art but a piece of Adam's bone." He paused. "Yes," he said, "The shamans told of a hunger winter so fierce a mother watching her family starve ignored the tribe's most sacred taboo, killing an owl and feeding it to her children."

"A sacrilege."

Brother Maurice nodded. "That night, and for many nights to come, the owls in the forest, angered by her transgression, began calling, calling Inuit names until only a few survived."

"Because of one dead owl," Sister Anne said. "No serpent? No apple?"

Brother Maurice grinned. "Mankind suffering for Eve's transgression."

"Don't tell Father Carlos."

"No way, Sister. No way. No words of mine could stop him from spreading ignorance."

Startled. Sister Anne asked, "Why do you say that?"

"Because it's true, Sister. Is it right to ask Indians to discard beliefs held sacred from the beginning of time? Are we doing God's work baptizing infidels who come to the mission only for food."

"You don't believe that."

"I do. And how can we ignore the tribes upriver? Aborigines who refuse our handouts? Infidels destined to burn in hell because they won't abandon what they believe. Aren't they as deserving of God's grace as the natives we baptize?"

"Why have you come to Santa Magdalena?

"I go where I am sent, Sister. An endless journey."

Sister Anne remained silent. Thinking. Brother Maurice was no theologian. And yes, years of poverty weakens faith. And yes, she never questioned her vocation before. And now, dear God, How could such doubts be overcome?

She turned to Brother Maurice, his face in shadow as he leaned forward to thrust his paddle into the water. Why was she so frightened? Afraid of ideas brought to Santa Magdalena by this troubled soul.

"Let's return to the mission," she said, digging her paddle deep. Pulling towards shore. "It's time to go back."

Yes. Such words accomplish nothing. She had other things to think about, like God forbid a child should die because she missed a symptom. At Santa Magdalena her life was fulfilled by what she did. Work was the meaning of her life.

"Why did you never become a priest?" she asked.

"Sister, where I come from education ends at twelve. I never disputed priests saying I was a hopeless case. Could barely read or write or remember my catechism. Holy orders were not for Canucks scratching out a living in the woods."

Silhouetted against the night sky on the river banks, the towering rain forest formed a narrow corridor leading upstream into the unknown. With each forward surge of the canoe Sister Anne peered ahead to see the first comforting glow of the Mission's lights. "You would have found a way," Sister Anne said. "If you wanted the priesthood."

Brother Maurice laughed. "True Sister. True."

"Why did you never try?"

"Sister, to some, the seminary was the road to glory. For me, cloistered behind stone walls, I would forever be looking up for a glimpse of the stars, hungry for the freedom of the forest, yearning for whatever is hidden over the horizon. In my heart I knew something alive in me would die if I were caged."

"Yet you seem eager to serve."

"In the only way I know, Sister. I am good with my hands. Happy. Alive. Give me a solid piece of wood and the right tools and I can work miracles."

Sister Anne agreed: Yes. That is so. Brother Maurice transformed the old mission into something substantial. Not eternal as the pyramids but built to endure a tropical jungle's ravages. Yes indeed, a "miracle" though she refused to degrade that word. Her "miracles" were antibiotics. Chemicals that cure. No more, no less.

What occurred that evening on the river re-appeared as a faded series of half-remembered images dissolving into each other. An incoherent film with the clarity of a deprived memory. I am good with my hands she recalled Brother Maurice saying, and she thought what an extraordinary thing for him to say, for she believed it was her hands touching flesh that restored life.

And then she recalled an enormous tree uprooted by the flood, looming out of the night's darkness, racing towards them in the fast moving current, bearing down on their canoe like a moving wall, leafy arms opened not to the sky in prayer, but sweeping over the muddy waters of the river like death itself.

Again she heard Brother Maurice shouting as the canoe capsized, her heart pounding, sinking down and down into blackness, lungs aching, greeting death before floating up to the world of the living to glimpse a dark horizon of unknown terrors and paralyzing fear. Enormous whirlpools formed concentric circles beneath the mist rising silently from the river. Then a huge hand reached down, weathered fingers groping in the darkness, lifting her out of the water as she howled a wild animal sound emerging from the depths of her soul, a rage of anger bellowed out of agonies accumulated in the years that came before, like the upwelling of a battered spirit in mortal distress. Then, slowly sinking, turning and twisting in weightless spirals, losing buoyancy as her lungs emptied, feeling an ecstatic exultation, a wild joy, she saw a strange figure sleeping in a bed of mud, head resting on his forearm, beard and long hair undulating in the current. Hovering over him, embraced by a happiness she had never known before, she felt drawn by a strange current carrying her down to the river bed. She surrendered to the force taking her down, arms outstretched, feeling herself slowly merge and absorbed into the mud contoured around the reclining form. Now beauty intensified, lingered like a melody as their bodies merged. She felt relaxed, tension draining through outstretched arms, vanishing through her fingertips as she experienced an enveloping peace that became an intense discharge of feeling. She felt her heartbeat slowing, the throbbing in her temples changing as her breathing stopped and a life-giving surge of blood pulsed through her body. She raised her head, her mouth opening without a word emerging to protest entrapment. Again she attempted to cry out, her soundless throat choking as her faltering strength formed in the depths of her being, forming a shout that failed to emerge. Then, exhausted, her energy vanished as she ceased to struggle, abandoning all effort, and peering up from the depths to the now strangely glittering surface of the river, she felt as if she had entered paradise.

When Sister Anne revived, bruised and naked on a beach amidst a tangle of flood-borne flotsam, she looked out over the river not knowing what she was searching for. The sun restored her sense of being alive, its heat brought new and luxurious feelings to a body never before exposed to a burning cloudless sky. She crawled under the sheltering shade of a fallen eucalyptus tree, aware of the hazardous tropical sun, covering herself with a garment of mud-spattered leaves that brought to mind Brother Maurice's poem.

"Fig-leafed wench," she said aloud, laughing, remembering the river, the enormous floating tree capsizing the canoe, and then drowning. Why am I alive she wondered, surprised, struggling to understand her feeling of well-being. Yes. It is true. She had never before felt so truly alive, so filled with joy, as she welcomed the return of that great good gift that was her life.

Next day, rescued by Father Carlos, she learned no trace of Brother Maurice or the canoe had been found. To search down stream on the flood-swollen river would risk more lives. This, said Father Carlos, in good conscience, "I can not permit."

SIXTEEN

Dear God! Was this my contrition? My penance? Living behind a double-locked apartment door, windows bolted and barred against intruders. What next? What next? Please God, why do you allow harassing door bells and obscene phone calls in the middle of the night? An existence I never imagined. Dante's circle of hell. Rumbling bus engines under my window mocking sleep. Grinding garbage truck compactors at dawn. Police sirens shrieking indifference to all human suffering. Yes, implacable evil stalks the streets. Santa Magdalena never prepared me for this.

Sister Anne eagerly accepted salvation. A room at the Irwins' far removed from New York City's violence.

Leg exercises and massages three times a day. Not a burdensome routine. Then accompanying Steve as he shuffled his steel-braced legs to the road. Tottering, muscles straining, swinging forward on crutches, step by step. A struggle ignored by Helen's cold fading beauty. Her indifference punctuated by silence. Yes. Silence was the language the Irwin's spoke. A mystery.

How gracefully elegant Helen walked, served a meal, raised a glass, held a cigarette. So self absorbed. Every morning her carefully prepared face was born anew. Created by a mind dedicated to appearance, silence and separate bedrooms. Yes. The Irwin's were a mystery beyond all she knew of people.

Steve lived in his head with words, incessantly reading and writing. Does he possess more than his determination to walk again? Lifting paralyzed legs on the exercise table, pushing against each heel, then pulling the leg forward, repeating the motions, could prevent atrophy. The most Steve should expect. Or was that it? One never knows.

Steve looked up one morning and smiled. Asking, "Don't you ever get tired of pulling and pushing my legs, day after day after day?" Anne paused, shaking her head. Disagreeing. "Mr. Irwin," she said, pumping both legs back and forth. "There is always a possibility, perhaps only a small chance, you will one day push back."

Steve Irwin never repeated the question again.

At night, Helen's untrespassed bedroom door was ignored by Steve who returned to his study with an unsmiling goodnight. Anne cleared the table, loaded the dishwasher, and escaped to an armchair in front of the fireplace where she luxuriated in the Irwin's library, re-entering the world of the imagination. Fog horns on the river often diverted her and she stopped reading to watch river mist roll beads of moisture down the window glass, like small human tears.

Turning from the window, Sister Anne began crying. Sobbing. Wondering - can a fraud be absolved? Enter heaven? Would confession restore hope in this world, or the next? Can words wash away sin? O Lord save me, grant me eternal rest. I've lost the faith that made life endurable. The girl I once was has become a woman. What life have I lived? Who have my hands touched? Stroked? Caressed? Who has my heart held, and lost? Yes. What have I become? My soul shrieks. Has anyone ever been held in my heart? Like the night, I do not stagnate. Do not stand still and sleep. I move. Yearning for morning, the dawn, the coming of the sun.

On the table next to Sister Anne's chair a schoolchild's notebook invited attention. Flamboyant handwriting, graceful loops and frequent underlinings, filled the open page. Anne turned to admire the penmanship. Indeed, recognizing what could only be a woman's hand. Helen's script.

Dear Diary:

"For more than seventy years recommended procedure for cancer of the breast has been radical mastectomy. Devised by William Halstead this operation removes the breast and areas to which malignant cells may have traveled through the lymph channels - the armpit glands - auxiliary nodes - and large chest muscles. Performed early enough this procedure eliminates the disease for the breast is gone and the chest wall is sealed by a skin graft taken from the thigh."

"IS THERE NO ALTERNATIVE?"

Dear Diary:

Today I feel as if I am in a play called "MY LIFE" while also seated in the audience watching my performance. Can't ignore the lump. Have an appointment tomorrow with a doctor. Doctor Z. The alphabet's terminal letter. Z recommends immediate tumor removal. Said nothing about mastectomy. The "M" word not used on initial visits. Discussed article I read.

Believes women's magazines do harm. Yes, knows about cobalt radiation. But remove Tumor first and we'll talk about what's next.

Dear Diary:

Recommended radical as most prudent. Radiation is statistically problematic. Not first choice. Surgeons must surge I guess. That is to say theirs is a cutting business! Hah!

Dear Diary:

Refused to sign a release unless it clearly states my refusal to submit to radical. Doctor Z explained lump probably benign. Most are. Promises to remove only the tumor and nothing but the tumor so help him God! His smiling secretary retypes the release. Are they playing games with my tit?

Dear Diary:

Standard operating procedures enable doctors to finesse decisions. For biopsy you're prepared for surgery under anesthesia with a signed release authorizing immediate breast removal if tumor is malignant. If eighty percent of all tumors are benign, how come they ask for consent before they know how critical the problem is?

Dear Diary:

Awoke this morning after only a lump removal. Found this gem of wisdom in the library: "Biopsy need not be immediately followed by radical surgery if evidence of malignancy appears in tissue sample. 363 cases show preliminary excision of lump involves no risk. Survival rates five to fifteen per cent higher when the major treatment is preceded by excision.

Method of treatment not decisive. More significant are the clinical stage of the disease when diagnosed, the patient's age and immunological strength. Ten year comparative study of all methods demonstrate a difference of less than one per cent in survival rates. Treatment by local excision and radiation equally effective."

Dear Diary:

> *A cheerful note: "No doubt many lives have been saved or prolonged by radical surgery.... 75% of women so treated die within fifteen years...."*

Dear Diary:

> *If there was an effective alternative to Radicals more women would more promptly seek help. If neither radiation nor surgery is a positive cure after cancer spreads beyond the breast, what's wrong with choosing only radiation?*

Dear Diary:

> *God save me from another magazine article or TV program. Smiling faces, testimonials, the inspirational: "I had one breast removed twelve years ago and six years later the other breast was removed along with my female organs and today I am living a full life and playing golf!*

> *Tell me, where does a big, busty broad throw up?*

Dear Diary:

> *"Definitely best sellers are books like: "Learning to live a full-life with cancer".... Choosing a procedure is a decision requiring facts. Not mindless, knee-jerk advice."*

Dear Diary:

> *Doctor Z told me not to wait.... time to cut! Situation is "imminent"... How soon is "imminent"? Cobalt versus radical alternatives undetermined. Age... extent of the disease.... type of cell.... condition of the affected nodes vital factors not yet fully evaluated.*

Dear Diary:

No malignant cells have penetrated the basement membrane. No invasion found. So why cut? Why? Why? Why? Possibility that the malignancy has metastasized is somewhere between one and thirty per cent.

Dear Diary or hopefully - Dear God:

Doctor gave me release to sign. To be or not to be mutilated? Is that the question?

SEVENTEEN

The weeks following Helen's surgery the Irwins lived together in chilled silence. There was nothing more to discuss. She was alive, feeling betrayed, rejecting the doctor's optimistic prognosis. Steve was attentive following the best advice for husbands in the worst of times. Helen drank and stared out the window at the greenery replacing all trace of winter. Steve wrote, and provided what little comfort and companionship his wife would accept. Helen slept during the day, reading at night. Her daily routine timed to evade contact, reluctantly acknowledging Steve's caring presence.

A month passed before Helen came downstairs, to sit at the fireplace wrapped in a patchwork comforter, her thin arms reaching out to poke at the flames. When Steve entered to add logs to the fire, she did not look up or say a word. He shared her silence.

Opening windows to air out the house, Helen welcomed the warm breeze carrying the first verdant odors of spring. Budding trees and bushes greened the garden, bringing new foliage that hid the neighboring houses. Soon they would have complete privacy. A world within a world without visitors. They were lone inhabitants of desolation.

Seated in his study, Steve ceased writing to listen to Helen pace the hardwood floor, pausing at the window, she gazed out at the river, immobile in the shadows, a nightgown pressed close to her scarred body. Waiting. Waiting. Waiting.

And then dancing. Feet shuffling, the floor creaking overhead as he looked up recalling her fierce concentration, her movements quickening as she stamped barefoot on the hard wooden floor. Her dancing soon reached a desperate climax before abruptly stopping. Then silence. Anticipation. Her footsteps slowly shuffled across the room as she stumbled onto the bed. An eerie sound, a recurring rhythm, a muffled, dull pounding signaled her distress. He rolled his chair to the stairs lowering himself down on to his hands, Helen's fierce movements calling him. With quick downward thrusts of his arms he climbed the stairs and entered her room.

Silhouetted against the window, Helen knelt on the bed, swinging forward, rocking back and forth in rhythmic supplication. With each forward thrust of her body her head pounded the wall. He crossed the room and pulled himself on to the bed, taking her in his arms.

Her body fought his embrace, moaning with each desperate lunge to the wall, rocking back and forth, gathering strength to break free of his grasp.

His grip tightened, rage convulsed her body as she twisted and turned and rolled across the bed, a furious animal trapped in his arms. She arched her back, sliding her hands between them, pushing against his chest. He held on.

She stiffened, accumulating power for another desperate lashing-out of arms and legs, her forehead pounding against his cheekbone, bloodying his nose, pain bringing tears as she struggled to free herself.

Drenched in sweat, chests heaving, their bodies merged in desperate grappling. He could feel their hearts beating behind a wall of flesh. Then, rising out of a well of misery, he felt a groan shuddering her body, exploding in his arms as she turned and twisted pulling them to the floor. Exhausted. Trembling. The cold hardwood chilled them as he reached up and pulled down the blanket covering their despair.

EIGHTEEN

Year after year, drink by drink, Helen subdued terrifying images. Alcohol muted all sensations in alternating cycles of pain and exultation. Her nightmare visions were washed away by dry Martinis. The mirror was her only solace, applying make-up a ritual, a passion. Blending the colors of her skin, underlining her eyes, working with light and shadow she created a haunting beauty that turned heads. The mirror was her canvas, her appearance a language she spoke with the authority of an artist in command of her medium.

She dressed well. Her courage applauded. She smiled at friends and drank alone in an effort to quiet her feeling of betrayal. She went to the city on Wednesdays. Shopping trips relieved the monotony of the house, the river, and the surrounding woodlands.

When told she never looked more beautiful she nodded, dismissing the compliment, concealing her anguish about the scar slashed across her chest.

Mutilation was the never-to-be uttered word dividing their bed with a barrier of chagrin maintained through years of drinking, hospitalizations and brief sobrieties.

Steve's sudden appearances, silently rolling across the floor on rubber-tired wheels startled her. "You're a damn ghost prowling the house," she said, trembling as she looked up from a book. "Get yourself a horn or a bell."

He rolled to the fireplace and closed the screen. His sweater frayed at the elbows, his trousers worn thin at the knees by leg braces.

"I'll try not to startle you."

She studied him slumped in his seat, staring at the flames, his face turned away, writing in his head. She opened a book, holding the pages, hands trembling, his noiseless appearance discomforting. Christ! Old lovable Lionel Barrymore rolled through a dozen movies in a wheelchair smiling, and never terrifying anyone so why be frightened by a husband wearing ruts in every carpet in the house?

An accusation on wheels. A millstone around her neck for ever and ever and ever, Amen. And no atonement possible. What the hell does he expect of her? Rub his forehead like James Cagney in the Miracle Worker? Off of the bed and on the floor a cripple walks to the bedroom door! A great scene. No doubt about that. But not for Helen. No way. She'll pass on miracles. Thank God for the nurse.

"I like Miss Bousquet," she said.

"She does her job."

"Doesn't intrude in our lives. Knows when to keep to herself."

Steve nodded. He wheeled from the fireplace, turning to the window. His face flushed.

"Don't get a chill," she said.

"Lucky to have her. Most therapists are muscle-brained," he said as he rolled towards the door.

"Where are you going?"

"To get a book."

"Which one?"

"On my desk."

She watched him wheel out of the room. The page she was reading blurred. She walked to the window. Seated on a stone bench on the terrace she saw a dark silhouette in the shadows staring at the lights across the river. Anne Bousquet sat there immobile as a statue watching and thinking. About what?

Steve wheeled on to the terrace to the steps leading down to the dock. He turned to look at the river, pointing at the stairway, pantomiming, his voice inaudible. Helen could not read the body language of arms and faces obscured in shadows. Anne walked to the stairs and looked at the steps. Steve's spontaneous burst of laughter made Helen wonder how long it had been since either she or Steve had laughed together.

Steve rolled his chair to the bench and turned to speak to Anne. Helen watched them, wondering, but not one gesture or word gave meaning to what she witnessed.

She turned from the window and gazed into the fireplace. The burning wood spiraled a black column of smoke up the chimney. Small tongues of flame curled under the logs as she jabbed them with a poker. Suddenly, exposed to air, the fire radiated a bright yellow heat that made her step back. She replaced the poker on its stand, warming herself, her hands thrust palms down towards the flames.

NINETEEN

Summer arrived with a truckload of two-by-fours stacked beside the stairs descending from the terrace to the river. The "Irwin Construction Company" began work constructing handrails. Steve measured and sawed wood, nailing railings to supporting posts. He built parallel handrails with diagonal wire bracing tensioned by turnbuckles. Supported by the railings, he lowered himself down to the water.

On the dock he removed both braces and massaged his legs. Then he lowered himself into the river, pushing out into deeper water, his powerful arms pulling him away from shore. He reached ahead, hands slicing beneath the surface, swinging down through the water, pulling himself forward as he again reached out, breathing easily, his mouth turning to one side with each stroke as the current carried him into the deep-water channel mid-stream.

He turned and swam parallel to shore, scissoring his legs as he moved through the water. He rolled on his back to look up at his home, waving at the slim figure on the terrace. He moved his hands chest high, treading water. Concentrating on his hips, thighs and legs, he felt the first slight flicker of sensation.

The water tasted brackish, the currents stirring the bottom raised mud that soon cleared in the fast-moving channel. Floating on his back, drifting, he accepted the pull of the current. He closed his eyes, arms extended, hands floating on the water, enjoying the warmth of the sun reflected off the river in long, dazzling glare streaks.

Good to be alive. He opened his eyes. The figure on the terrace vanished. The house seemed small, and no doubt the red slate roof could be seen from the opposite shore. Yes. The bushes on the hillside above his dock needed clearing.

Someday. Soon.

He looked upstream. He had floated past the lighthouse where the river narrowed between the highlands. He recalled walking to that point many times. Now more than a mile from shore, across from an old barge rotting on the beach, he maintained an easy rhythm, conserving strength, swimming against the current, watching the dock and the house recede as he drifted downstream. He stared at the barge. It now seemed smaller, aground on the beach. His stroke quickened, digging his arms down deep fighting the strong current flowing out to sea.

Then, he rested, waiting for water to clear his eyes.

Abeam of the barge. No nearer to shore. The ebb tide stronger. The house, the dock, the lighthouse receding. He could swim for hours without reaching the beach. He now swam at an angle to the current towards the barge. The current weakened as he moved into shallow water. Progress improved. He counted strokes. At one hundred he rested and studied the barge. Yes, it now seemed higher on the beach. Another hundred strokes. Yes, he could see more of the barge. A hundred more strokes, and then another, and when he looked again he saw sand and rocks washed-up under the rotting timbers of the abandoned barge. He floated on his back and closed his eyes. Five hundred more yards to go.

He swam, each stroke bringing him closer to the beach. Turning parallel to the river bank he moved slowly upstream. Now he saw on the dock, a thin figure shading her eyes with one hand.

Anne cupped her hands to shout. She dove into the water swimming out to him.

In chest-deep water he touched the river bottom with his feet. Arms outstretched, head and shoulders above the surface, he tried to stand.

"Are you OK?", Anne shouted.

With a sweep of his arms he paddled closer to shore, into shallow water. He straightened his legs, pushing down against the river bottom, his upper body buoyant. He realized when swimming to the barge he had kicked his legs.

He stood upright supported by the buoyancy of the water walking towards shore, the water receding to his waist, the weight supported by his legs increasing as he walked to the beach. Anne swam to him. He waved at her, losing balance, falling forward, swimming away, rolling on his back, laughing as she followed him. He walked into deeper water its buoyancy holding him upright as he thrust his legs into the mud moving away from her, stumbling over the bottom.

"Take it easy," she shouted.

He stepped into shallower water, laughing, the weight on his legs increasing until suddenly his muscles collapsed and he fell down into the river

surfacing to cough and shout and wave at Anne. She
followed as he dove beneath the water, swimming
under her, surfacing as she circled back towards
him. He waited as her arms moved out in a graceful
breaststroke. Then he dove down swimming over the
muddy bottom, rolling on his back to watch her body
silhouetted against the blazing arc of the sun. Anne
swam past him as he scissored his legs moving into
deeper water.

She tread water as he surfaced. Her hair streaming
behind her.

"Don't overdo," she said.

He swam towards shore, standing when his feet
touched bottom. She followed emerging from the
water her bathing suit clinging to her thin, girlish
body.

She held out her arms.

"When maintaining balance your arms are
important," she said. "Take care when reaching. Arms
pull you forward. Keep them close to your side."

He grinned.

"There are only a few rules."

"Not today. Please. No more. Not today."

She swam to shore, sitting on the sand, water
splashing at her waist. She gathered a handful of small
stones. Then began skipping them over the surface of
the river.

"Where did you learn that?"

She threw another stone skipping it over the waves.

"I was a tomboy."

"I should have known."

She laughed. "I skipped stones, climbed trees,
pitched hay. Grew up on a farm."

"And milked cows?"

She smiled. "Let's swim".

He followed, matching his strokes with hers, swimming parallel to the beach, the current carrying them downstream to the barge. He felt buoyant, water flowing past his body, hips and legs scissoring, strength increasing. He turned on his back floating while Anne treaded water beside him.

"Enough?" he asked.

She nodded. They swam to shore. The deep-throated blast of a ship's horn maneuvering midstream blared as he waited for her to join him. Then he heard another horn signaling the departure of a tugboat steaming from behind the breakwater across the river. Anne raised her hand to wave him on. He turned away, and when he looked across the muddy water towards shore he saw Helen Irwin watching them from the dock.

TWENTY

Joining words together was Steve Irwin's sacrament. The jangling of his typewriter intensified Helen's discomfort evoking the thought: "There must be more to life than this?"

There must be.

But there was not. In the tormenting hours before dawn Helen Irwin turned in bed to stare out the window recalling feelings that once gave her life coherence. Feelings directed at someone or some purpose. Now these feelings were blunted. Hopes dissolved in drink.

The core of herself was beyond resurrection. She had once been whatever she felt like becoming and now she had lost all sense of this self. The ultimate terror.

Non-existence.

No longer ingénue, supporting player, star, or performer of "promise" applauded by critics and a discerning public. She was not this any more than she was wife or mother.

So what was she?

Alone. Alone.

Helen never learned how to defeat loneliness and having lost the center of her being her solitude was filled with thoughts made homeless by that most terrible of all deaths.

The death of self.

As the dawn grayed the horizon across the river she pulled the blanket to her chin, shivering in the morning chill. Yes, I am dead, truly dead, and with these words I thee wed in an effort not to lose those few bedded moments holding on to that last pulsation called love. 'Le petit mort' the French say. The little death that for me was an instant of life split into an infinity of longing. Keeping a brave face a necessity, and when the made-up face of my persona faltered or frowned or mumbled a speech it brought catastrophe. So if you can't conquer life with your cunt, what's the alternative? Like an oyster never yielding a pearl worth holding up to the light, I gestated my art, not in words and struttings on stage, but in a futile struggle to distill out of my emotions, each and every honest performance, in a lifetime asking help from nobody but myself.

Little Miss Nobody, nowhere. Not in ten thousand and one hotel rooms or airplanes or trains. Not in fifty cities. Not in one hundred theaters or restaurants or taxicabs or chauffeured limousines. Not even in this oversized barn of a home did I ever feel I was someone who was somewhere I belonged.

A lifetime of dislocations and phone calls and letters that never arrived, or if they did, remained unanswered until all possibility of a human connection had been lost. Yes, I paid little attention to what truly mattered, frittering away my love, my spirit, my beauty.

And yes, yes indeed, "The pencil of God has no eraser."

She slid out from under the bedcovers and walked to the window, wiping condensation from the glass, listening to the mechanical staccato of a typewriter machine-gunning words over the difficult terrain of a blank white page.

The infantry of Steve Irwin's mind advancing line by bloody line, knowing neither retreat nor victory as they marched to inevitable failure.

She pulled her nightgown over her head and studied her body in the full-length mirror. A slender silhouette, narrow-waisted, long legs and arms with just the right amount of feminine width at the hips. She stared at herself grateful for shadows concealing disfigurement. Then she put on her brassiere adjusting the heavy rubber form that restored her bust. She was told she gave too much importance to something that made no difference to anybody but herself. Idiots! As if what anybody thought, mattered. Part of herself had been disposed of, disfigured, mutilated, and no kind words could ever wash away her rage.

Never.

She dressed and went downstairs to the kitchen pouring a cup of coffee from the pot on the stove. She lit a cigarette, throwing the match into a sink filled with unwashed dishes. At the window, she sipped coffee looking at the garden. A dry summer. The parched grass displayed burn-streaks extending to the shade trees. The months without rain seemed as arid as the desert in her heart.

She descended the cellar stairs to a basement under wooden beams spanning the foundation walls. She switched on a light above her workbench, the unshaded bulb illuminating a row of glazed pottery, bags of clay, a kiln, and a potter's wheel holding an unfinished urn.

She dipped her hands into a bucket of water under the wheel, wetting the urn, slowly revolving the circular platform as the clay absorbed water, becoming pliable to her touch. She turned on the motor, the urn rotating and slowly changing shape between her fingers. Again she wet her hands, reaching into the mouth of the urn, thinning its side with her palms.

She lowered and then raised her hands, shaping the clay, raising the sides before turning them inward, narrowing the neck in a graceful curve sweeping up from a wide, flat base. It was as if her spirit flowed through her fingertips. Her hands applying delicate pressures, shaping the spinning clay, creating a form delighting her eye. Her hands created a world of order and beauty and perfect symmetry.

If only she could live by her hands.

She switched-off the motor, the inertia of the spinning wheel turning the urn, the pressure of her palms gradually slowing rotation. Then she lit a cigarette, and raising the cover of the kiln, pulled out a bottle of vodka and poured herself a drink.

Perfection! A blue glaze baked into the clay would complete this masterpiece. She didn't ask more than to sit peacefully and sooth her nerves with a drink. If only she could focus her mind on her fingertips, her pottery would soon be fine enough to sell.

Yes, a dark blue glaze would be perfect. Baking in colors at the right time and temperature is the trick. She slid a cutting wire under the base of the urn, separating it from the potter's wheel. Then, she lowered it into the kiln placing the damp clay form on a metal rack above rows of gas jets, closing the kiln with an iron lid.

Now that she controlled her drinking a new career was possible. She does know colors. Bake the clay with the right combination of pigments and you create extraordinary effects, like a rich ocean blue darkening into a black angry sea. Add a touch of white streaking the blue to the softness of a misty sky. I know everything about pastels, shading an exquisite range of subtle effects, the clay acquiring a translucent quality, making inanimate objects come alive! Yes. Right here at my fingertips is salvation! Colors! Colors no one's ever imagined before. A red that explodes across the room when you turn on the light. Like Van Gogh's Sunflowers, there's never been a canvas that could contain the colors in my head. The blue flowing under the Bridge of Arles. Who ever saw a blue like that? And sunlight? You've got to feel the hot sun in your gut before you can see what Van Gogh saw blazing across a landscape.

Yes, I love all my fantastic colors. Like Van Gogh's beauties.

From the shelf over the workbench she took down the timing clock and turned the winding key, advancing the hour hand. She adjusted the temperature of the kiln and turned on the gas.

Placing a ball of soft clay on the wheel, she began to sing as she resumed working. The clay revolving between her palms came alive as she varied the pressure shaping the pliant mass slowly rising on the turntable. The dark blur of the spinning clay gradually became a graceful form between her fingers. She loved simple shapes, gentle curves, sweeping arcs bending to her will as the walls became thinner. Yes, it was too much to expect that our lives could be shaped by our hands. So we work with clay. Or words.

One day she would create a great masterpiece! A tall, graceful vase with thin sides delicately rising from a small circular base in sweeping curves narrowing and then bending like a poem in space. And yes, yes. In the center of this beauty, this perfection, she would someday find that remarkable creation that was her imperishable soul.

TWENTY ONE

Exhausted by a day in New York, Anne slept on the train. A disturbing dream awakened her anxiety about the Irwins. Riding along the river, she gazed across the water at the granite cliffs on the opposite shore, rock Palisades extending upriver to the highlands, with the ominous shadows of an early summer evening darkening her mood. Yes, the Irwins were lost in a way she did not understand. And yes, they had courage, enduring a misery that would never end.

The train entered the tunnel downstream from the Irwin's home. Her window blackened for a moment and when the train emerged into daylight she saw the narrow highway running parallel to the tracks, crowded with cars parked on the side of the road. She turned to look out the window, straining to see the roof of the house beyond the cliff next to the railroad station.

She stepped on to the platform and hurried across the wooden ramp to the blacktop road running up the hill that blocked her view of the house. When she reached the crest of the hill, she saw firemen, faces grimed from smoke, draining hoses, unscrewing brass nozzles, loading them on a truck. She choked on the sour, acrid odor of burnt wood and plaster wetted down with water and foam as she entered the garden crowded with ladders, axes and hoses. And now, as in her dream, she walked from the road stumbling over hoses, unaware of the firemen staring at her as she heard a far away voice, an unfamiliar voice repeating words she could not understand. She walked through the crowd of men who stepped aside as she approached, mute faces turning away from her as she questioned them, unstated words on her lips, terrible questions trapped in the tight fist clutching at her heart.

She heard someone speak of an explosion as she was led away from the ruin, and looking down, she saw her shoes blackened by soot, a darkening stain covering the green lawn. Then two firemen carried a black canvas bodybag out to the road as someone grasped her arm, turning her away from horror.

How familiar it all seemed as she wandered among the firemen disassembling ladders and grappling hooks, black rubber coats opened wide in the summer heat. Where once there had been a house there was now only a large space open to the sky, an odd gap in the treeline overlooking the river.

Then she recalled her dream as she staggered through the crowd to the blackened foundation walls, where, just as in her vividly remembered dream, she saw Steve Irwin, without crutches, or leg braces, walking back and forth on the charred floor timbers scavenging in the burned-out rubble of his home.

About The Author

After a 42 year career as a writer-director of many award-winning films and television programs, Norman Weissman has written two novels and a memoir. Determined to oppose the silence in which lies become history, the author makes his reply in Art to tell of all he has witnessed during more than half a century of filming at home and overseas.

He lives in rural Connecticut with his wife Eveline, and their little dog Suzie.